Broken Wall

Baland Iqbal

Toronto
2022

Published by
Baland Iqbal
Toronto, Canada

Broken Wall by *Baland Iqbal*
Second Edition Published in 2022 by *Meraj Publishing House, Canada*
Translated by *Jozair Baland*
Edited by *Gordon A. Long*
Cover design & formatting by *Nabin Karna*
Cover Photo by *Ahmed Janahi* with use of
http://www.pptbackgrounds.org/

This is a work of fiction. Names, characters, businesses, places, events, locales, and incidents are either the products of the author's imagination or used in a fictitious manner. Any resemblance to actual persons, living or dead, or actual events is purely coincidental.

Dedicated to my dreams,

A world where there are no differences based on color, race, or religion.

"Our separation of each other is an optical illusion of consciousness."

~ Albert Einstein

Contents

Chapter 1

Time: About 4:30 pm
Date: November 6, 2016
Place: Shah Faisal Colony, Karachi, Pakistan

"Grab him! Grab that son of a bitch! He's been using abusive language for our Prophet! How dare this bastard have the courage?" Idrees yelled as he raced like a wild animal behind a man wearing a bright white *kurta shalwar*.

His 9-year-old son, Usman, slipped his finger from Idrees's hand and scampered to a broken wall nearby. As he peeked around the corner of the wall, his gaze fell upon his father, still chasing the man dressed in white. He cringed as he remembered the way his father, only a couple of minutes before, had grabbed the man and attacked him, before the man jerked his hand out of his attacker's grasp and tried desperately to run away.

Rab Nawaz, sitting nearby with his knees folded on the wall, overheard the commotion. He drew the attention of another friend sitting nearby. "Oy, Kallo. Who is this bastard that Idrees is trying to catch?"

Kallo looked but didn't see anything.

Rab Nawaz sighed in annoyance. "Not that side, stupid. Look that way, there, where Idrees is running."

He pointed Kallo's face into the right direction, towards the road crossing. "See, over there! Near Neakoo's restaurant, where our friend Idrees is running to catch some guy. See him? Yes, that guy, the one wearing a *shalwar*. Did you see him? Idrees just shouted that the guy insulted our Prophet!"

He let go of Kallo and shouted to Idrees, "Get ahold of him, the bum, and make sure he doesn't get away. Don't let the pimp get away!"

Kallo now began to shout similar comments.

Rab Nawaz bellowed, "O brother Idrees, see that he doesn't escape!"

Kallo and Rab Nawaz ran towards the road crossing, shrieking profanities and curses. Taking a shortcut, they scaled the six-foot fence and ran through the centre of the park to overtake Idrees, aiming to catch the man who had badmouthed the Prophet and initiated Idrees' infuriation.

Other people sitting in the park stared with concern towards Rab Nawaz and Kallo, trying to understand the situation. Soon a massager waiting for his client, two Mullahs sitting on the grass and about six labourers waiting to be hired began to follow Rab Nawaz and Kallo, also trying to help Idrees.

In no time, most of the people in the park were trailing Idrees to help him punish the blasphemer.

The confused and fearful man in white turned for a moment to catch a glimpse of the menacing mob catching up to him. Turning back, he slammed into a banana seller's cart, his head smashing into the concrete road. He scrambled up and tried to resume his escape, but failed, stumbling. He rolled over and lay there, injured.

Idrees leaped onto him and punched his face several times. Rising, he kicked the man's stomach fiercely.

The man rolled over, his shalwar red with blood, writhing in pain like a crippled dog.

Idrees, raging with anger, grabbed hold of his leg and dragged him, shouting at the mutilated man.

"Speak, *kafir ki olad*! Tell us what you uttered."

The man only groaned in pain.

Rab Nawaz and Kallo reached the area and, no questions asked, started beating and kicking the man. They continued thrashing him mercilessly for quite some time.

The man was half dead. Crying in pain, he shrieked hysterically, "I said nothing! All I said was that Mohammad is not my prophet! I am Christian, and my prophet is Jesus!"

"You bastard, you took his name in vain once more. He is the prophet of every single man in the world! How dare you utter his name?" Kallo struck him once more. "He is the prophet of the entire world!" As he shouted, he booted his victim hard in the stomach.

The taller of the two Mullahs among the crowd hollered, "This bastard is committing blasphemy! An agent of Jews, a sweeper! Son of a Christian. Such bastards are all over. In Islam, the punishment for blasphemy is death!"

In no time, the whole crowd began kicking and hitting the poor man, now writhing in a pool of his own blood.

Idrees was the main antagonist, cracking a brick onto the head of the man in white and shouting, "Oy, Kallo! Go bring us some petrol."

"Right away, Idrees. We're going to send this filthy one to hell right now."

Kallo rushed to a nearby mechanic's shop and grabbed a tin of petrol. Idrees shouted to the mob. "Give way, motherfuckers! This hound of a man is going to be burnt, right here! Nobody will ever dare to say that Prophet Mohammad is not our prophet."

Kallo threw petrol all over the man, leaving him soaked.

The man was begging for help from the crowd gathered around him. He begged for his life in the name of the Prophet and in the name of God.

Right then Idrees threw three lighted matches at him.

The man made a final, aching effort to get up and run, but flames engulfed him. His cries and writhing movements were horrific. He was trying to run with his body enveloped in flames, but his movements were but the swirling of flames punctuated with shrieks and hissing as the flames consumed him.

People continued to watch, and in the midst of the hellish play, the man died.

Finally only his remains were left: a charred body and the smell of burnt flesh. After observing the gory drama, the crowd slowly dissipated. Only a few hung around, making videos of the event with their phones.

Idrees stepped out of the crowd and spat on the burnt body of the man. Then he turned to Kallo and Rab Nawaz. "Now that dog will burn in hell forever. Let's go from here. This will become a police case."

Hearing this, Kallo roared, "What police case? He committed blasphemy and the punishment for blasphemy is death! We'll burn down the police station if they dare register the case. Are the police dogs oblivious to that?"

Idrees nodded. "All right, we'll just leave for now." Then he looked around and asked, "Oh, you fools, where's Usman?"

"Who's Usman?" Kallo asked.

"My son. Who else? He was with me when I was yelling at this son of a bitch," he muttered, pointing towards the charred body. "That bastard turned my head. Now tell me, did you see my son?"

"He'll be somewhere here. We'll find him. Now, tell me who this bastard was." Rab Nawaz asked Idrees.

"All right, my friend. I'll tell you. It's a long tale, and we had been arguing for a long time, but this time he crossed the limit. That is why he died burning."

All of a sudden Rab Nawaz nudged Idrees. "Oy, there's Usman!" He pointed towards the broken wall nearby.

"Oy, Usman. Get over here." Idrees shouted, waving his hand.

But the boy stood there, staring at the smoke rising out of the scorched body of the man burnt to death.

Idrees again shouted, "Oh Usman, come here."

Usman turned his head towards his father, regarding him with the same horror. All of a sudden he spun away and vomited on the ground.

Chapter 2

Time: 8:30 am
Date: November 7, 2016
Location: Kabul, Afghanistan

When the phone rang, Professor Wahidi stopped typing on his computer, walked over and picked it up. "Oh, Nazir. Yes, I'm leaving for the university in ten minutes. I'll meet you at the news stand."

He hung up the phone and walked back to the computer. He quickly read Sania's last message in his chatbox:

Sania: ...sir, I still don't get it. Who would you blame for human barbarism? Is it in their hereditary character... or where they grew up...in a world of pseudo-civilization?

Wahidi: Sania, this is a long discussion. It's eight in the morning here and probably midnight for you. Why don't we leave this one for later?

Sania: Oh, sure. See you later, professor.

Wahidi put his bag over his shoulder and regarded the room. Books were scattered around: on the bed, on the floor and all over the carpet. His bed sheet was crumpled and the pillow was creased.

His eyes fell onto a book lying on his desk, *Heretic*, by controversial Somali-born Dutch-American author, Ayaan Hirsi Ali. Wahidi thought about her life at the top of the Taliban's hit-list.

He pushed the volume into his bag and glanced into the mirror as he was leaving. His hair was spread across his head in an untidy mix of black and white. His scruffy, short beard had the same blend of colour. His blue eyes, light skin colour and prominent forehead gave him a typical Afghani look. He dragged a comb through his hair and tucked in his shirt.

He walked into the garage and put his car into gear, but before he started driving, he heard the doorbell sound from inside the house. Wahidi glanced at his wristwatch and muttered, "Who'd show up at this time?"

He shrugged, opened the car door, and walked to his main gate…nobody was there. Then he noticed an envelope on the sidewalk near the door. Surprised, he kneeled down and picked it up, locking the door and coming back to his room.

Inside the envelope he found a small slip of paper, written in Pashto:

Professor, clean up your act…

… or your fate won't be pleasant.

Wahidi crumpled it up and tossed it aside. He mocked the note with a wry smile. "Clean up your act. Ha."

He looked around the messy room and muttered to himself. "What could be worse than this? If she hadn't been murdered, my life would never have turned into this mess."

He opened a bedside drawer and pulled out a pistol, tucking it into his coat. His hand brushed against a pen in the same pocket, and he pulled both of them out, placing the gun and the pen on the desk in front of him.

It reminded him of *Heretic*. Just like the differences in Muhammad's Mecca life and his Medina life. One was spiritual and full of peace while the other full of war and violence.

He shrugged, smiled and put both the gun and the pen into the leather bag beside *Heretic.* He walked back to the garage, got into his car and drove out.

Once he crossed the street and reached the highway, he found the torn city of Kabul surrounding him, the result of the 15-year-long civil war. The streets were congested, and the gutters, full of filth, turned the road into multiple pools of mud.

At one time the drive to the university took him ten minutes. Today the patty sellers and horse-cart drivers wandering along the road made it forty minutes.

When he found the Tahsellat-e Ali Islam sign on the eminent blue building, Wahidi took a deep breath of relief. Now, the bare path would reshape itself into a paved road. Here, the houses on each side of the street were traditional Afghani ones. These houses differentiated in size rather mercilessly. Some were miniature, made up of sludge and dirt. The windows were so small that from a distance, one could only see darkness inside. The big houses were like bungalows, with wide windows and high walls, dressed with colourful glass that gave them a mosaic look, mainly using the colours red and blue.

In front of the Markazi Movie Invasion signboard, he approached the bus terminal. It was crowed as always. It sported many more signboards in English. Construction around the terminal continued at a rapid pace.

Wahidi ignored the sound of vehicles and busy construction work around him. His mind was brimming with thoughts about the historical evolution of this part of the world. He felt, amidst the traffic, as if he was also imprisoned in time—like the current state of Afghanistan. His car was on a road of cement while his mind was on a road of history.

Seeing the autumn bushes along the sides of the road, Wahidi's mind raced to 300 BC, travelling to the time of Chandragupta Maurya, one of the most patriotic and popular rulers of India.

A thousand years ago there were beautiful spring bushes at this spot, bringing him to 500 BC, the time of Cyrus and Alexander the Great, a time when Afghanistan was one of the flourishing countries of the world.

As fumes from the tandoor stands carried into the open car window, he smiled and thought of Zoroastrian Afghanistan, back when God was personified with fire.

He glanced at the construction being done over the buried necropolis and was reminded of the Islamic Afghanistan from 622 Hijra.

He felt relieved when he drove near a newly finished structure, now reminded of the modern Afghanistan of Amanullah Khan and King Zahir Shah, known for creating the dream of a new nation.

When dust from the tall and crumbling residences fell into his car, he rolled up the windows and muttered, "Oh, it looks like Talibani times have started."

As he thought about the last fifteen years of Hamid Karazi and Ashraf Ghani, the two rulers of Afghanistan who never knew what their destiny would be, Wahidi searched for Nazir, who usually could be found reading the newspaper in one of the restaurants nearby. But today he didn't see Nazir anywhere.

As he pulled out his cellphone to ring Nazir, he noticed an incoming call. He heard Nazir's familiar voice, unusually anxious.

"I'm at the university and we have some trouble. Stay where you are or go to some friend's house. Just don't come here until I call you."

Before Wahidi could ask what was wrong, Nazir hung up.

Annoyed, he shrugged and put the phone into his pocket and reversed his car into the restaurant's parking lot.

Chapter 3

Time: 10:30 p.m.
Date: November 6, 2016
Location: Mississauga, Canada

Sania: Oh, sure. See you later, professor.

After Sania sent the message to Professor Wahidi, she signed off Facebook but kept looking at the screen, deep thought. She then clicked on the camera icon and looked at herself on the screen. She had come back from university three hours ago. After dinner, she worked on her assignments for an hour or two, and then, tired, she chatted online with professor Wahidi.

After coming back from university, she didn't get time to refresh herself or change clothes. Her hairdo, however, was in place. The eyeliner she had put on in the morning looked quite attractive. Her face looked tired due to the day's work, so using the camera of the computer as a mirror, she took her lipstick from her purse nearby and applied it.

She next took out her lipstick pencil and shaped the ends of her lips. She then dabbed on a touch of face powder.

Satisfied with her makeup, she posed before the mirror and took a few pictures of herself. She chose one and attached it to a Skype message on her cellphone.

Miss you!

She got a message back from Daleep almost immediately.

I miss you, too!

Before she could reply, another message appeared on the screen.

Looking gorgeous!

Sania replied, *I feel like meeting you!*

Immediately, Daleep responded, *Come over now. We'll meet at Dixie's 24-Hour Starbucks.*

What do I tell Mom?

Isn't she asleep yet?

Dad isn't home. He's gone to his friend's place. Once Mom goes to sleep, I can get to Starbucks, probably within half an hour. See you then!

After typing this, Sania signed out.

* * *

Half an hour later Sania and Daleep were sitting in the corner of a Starbucks, facing each other comfortably and gazing into each other's eyes. After sipping coffee for a while, Sania, fluttering her eyelashes, fixed her gaze on Daleep and asked, "Now, tell me the answer to the question I asked earlier."

With the same adoring look in his eyes, Daleep replied, "My answer is the same one I told you in class this morning. Don't you remember what I wrote?"

Sania smiled coquettishly, "I bet now you're going to start a medical dissertation to make me understand."

Daleep imitated her tone. "Yes! Exactly, as you make me understand things using your psychological terminology."

"All right, let's start."

"All right, now listen," Daleep, like a professor, took out a pen, picked up a restaurant napkin and drew four circles onto it.

Pointing to one circle he said, "This is Canada and its snowy clouds."

Then, he drew a couple of small circles above it.

"Snow was falling on our heads when we first met in the upper lobby of the university."

Daleep made sketches of two people and pointed to one. "That one's you and the other one's me, when we met for the first time."

After completing the sketches he asked, "Do you remember, Sania?"

Sania looked curiously at sketches. "Oh yes, I think I do!"

Then, in his deep, Punjabi voice, he said, "Now, look over here."

Sania put her face into her palms, looked up and smiled. "Show me."

"When, on that fateful day, our eyes looked into each other's, a silent message was conveyed between us." He drew two parallel lines leading from the eyes of one of the figures into the brain of the other.

Sania, her eyes romantically half closed, asked, "And what was that message?"

"Oh, you know it well!" Daleep said in the same tone. "What was that message? Don't pretend."

He grinned and made two sketches of cupids in front of their eyes.

"The message comes out from the eyes and goes straight into the mind and tells us that this girl and boy have fallen in love. Their minds found that something new had happened and soon realized that it was the sweet feeling of love between the two. The feeling of peace pervades all, and in no time, trillions of neutrons and transmitters start to emit themselves: dopamine, serotonin, and norepinephrine."

Daleep made numerous small blots with the tip of his pen on the heads of sketches. Once he was finished, he continued.

"It doesn't matter how heavy it was snowing in Toronto that day. These flying hormones attack the sweat glands of boy and girl and they start sweating. Even if they are lying still, these hormones make the heart beat as fast as if they were running on a treadmill.

"In a situation like this, it does not matter if they're having, say, delicious food in a Chinese restaurant. The two do not feel hungry at all.

"In a situation like this, it doesn't matter how many snowy clouds hang overhead. The two of them feel a clear, blue sky and wish to gaze at the full moon and count the stars."

As Daleep started counting, Sania stopped him. "What if these are signs of depression? By the way, Doctor, there is another disease in psychology and we call it schizophrenia. Aren't you mixing the two?"

She added, "I'll tell you about the psychology of love." She picked up the tissue paper on which Daleep was making sketches, rolled it into a paper ball, and then, one eye closed, aimed for the dustbin and threw it in.

Daleep, with a wink of an eye said, "It involves the sex hormones too."

Sania, with mischievous stress, said, "Okay, Professor." Then she became serious. "By the way, does it matter if the girl is Pakistani, Urdu-speaking and from an Ahmadi family, and the boy is from India, Punjabi-speaking and from a Sikh family?"

"It doesn't matter here in Canada, but in Pakistan and India it's different." He raised his hands in mock defense as if he was about to get a good beating.

First Sania laughed, but then she got serious again. "It makes a difference here in Canada too, you know. It makes a big difference."

Daleep became serious as well. He held Sania's hand in both of his own and said with emotion, "This dopamine hormone, which secretes from the brain when two love birds look into each other's eyes…Sania Miss, this is our lifesaver hormone. When it secretes, one does not bother about religion or origin and cares about absolutely nothing.

"It only creates love and the will to fight until the end. It's a very strong hormone. And you know, Sania, life is created with love…and I love you, Sania, and I cannot live without you."

Saying this, he looked into her eyes and slowly embraced her.

They both closed their eyes and were lost in each other.

Outside of the coffee house it was snowing. From the sky to the earth, there was no religion at this moment. No language, no nationality, nothing but the serenity of love, and love only.

In the season of extreme cold, Daleep and Sania were sweating profusely and their heartbeats were rising…

Is this only the effect of dopamine and serotonin? Or is it something else…something that can't be seen?

Sania opened her eyes and looked around the coffee house as if she was searching for something…only to find the love of Daleep.

She hugged him more tightly and closed her eyes.

Chapter 4

Time: 10 am
Date: November 7, 2016
Location: Shah Faisal Colony, Karachi, Pakistan

Bakhtawar regarded Usman with a worried look on her face. "He hasn't been sleeping well and awakens every hour, shrieking and puking. He hasn't eaten anything, Idrees."

"I'll call the doctor here in a while. He'll give him a shot and he'll get well soon." Idrees scratched his back and let out a big yawn. "Looks like there's going to be a storm today!"

He glanced at the sky and walked into the bathroom.

Just as Idrees shut the door to the bathroom, the thuds of someone banging on the front door echoed throughout the small house.

Bakhtawar shouted, "I'm coming, I'm coming! What're you going to do, break it?"

She released the latch of the door, coming face to face with several policemen.

"Is Idrees home?" An officer said in an authoritative voice.

Bakhtawar, stunned, asked, "Uh…why do you want to meet him?"

"Oy, he burnt a guy alive. There is Section 402 charge against him for murder." The officer said with the same tone.

"He's not home at the moment," She lied, looking at the bathroom out of the corner of her eye. "Once he's back, I'll tell him."

"Don't tell him. Just send him to the police station." The officer said, swinging his baton in his hand. "His name is on the list of the mob who killed the guy yesterday. We'll need a statement from him."

After saying this, the police walked away.

Bakhtawar bolted the door and began to rap on the bathroom door, shouting, "Idrees, get out! The police were here!"

"I'm *coming*, I'm *coming!*" Idrees replied from inside. After a few seconds, he opened the door, rubbing his neck with a towel. "What's the fuss?"

"The police came! They used your name and said that you murdered someone." Bakhtawar said anxiously.

"Must be because of yesterday's episode. Don't worry, it was a case of blasphemy. Once the police hear they'll be pretty scared themselves. Didn't I tell you last night about the Christian *kafir* committing blasphemy about our beloved Prophet and the crowd of people that killed him?" He looked into her eyes and said, "It was a sin. The Molvi Salimullah of our area told us to keep an eye on this kinda stuff. Hold on, let me call him before I go to the police station so he can get me off. Don't worry about it."

Saying this, Idrees, called Molvi Salimullah and said, "Yeah, cops were over here, along with two or three other guys. Yes, he harassed my wife. Okay, yeah. Thank you."

He turned to Bakhtawar.

"Job's done. Molvi Salimullah called a religious school and he's going to come with about thirty or forty students to the police station. Now we'll teach them a lesson. How dare they harass a woman?"

Idrees went into his room and came out with a religious cap on his head and a scarf given to him by the Molvi Salimullah around his neck.

The noise of the drawers woke Usman. Seeing Idrees, he started screaming hysterically, half awake. "*No*! Don't burn me!" He began to shriek. "*Fire!*"

He started flailing all over the bed writhing and slapping his clothes as if he was on fire.

Idrees ran up to his son and grabbed him. "What happened, son? What's wrong?"

Usman shook himself free from Idrees' hands and hid behind his mother. "Mom, save me! Save me!" he screamed, eyes full of fear.

Bakhtawar cradled her son. "Oy, what happened to Usman?"

Idrees scratched his chin. "Oh, don't worry. I'll get Dr. Manzoor to give him some medicine when I come back. Probably got a bit scared after last evening."

Idrees walked out of the house towards the mosque to see Molvi Salimullah.

He had hardly crossed the street when Rab Nawaz, standing at the corner, shouted his name and came running to him.

Gripping his shoulder, he whispered. "Oy, Idrees, last night's case has taken a serious turn. The police took Kallo. He gave out the names of a couple of people and your name is at the top, man. You better disappear. It seems like a risky case."

Idrees's his face twisted with anger. "To hell with them! Let the buggers touch me. I've got an entire mosque behind me, a mosque. Know what a mosque is? A militia! Who do you think I am, Kallo? We'll blow up the entire station.

"Does it look like it was a personal matter? It was all for Islam! Listen, brother. Keep this in your mind." Idrees stared at Rab Nawaz and spat on the ground in anger. "We can sacrifice our lives for our Prophet's honour if we have to. These idiot policemen, do they have any idea of this honour? Do they even know what it means…pork eaters, bastards, living on bribes, *kafir saaley…*"

Before Idrees could finish, a Pajero Jeep and a white Mercedes pulled up, blowing dust into their faces. A few long-bearded Molvis came out of them and respectfully shook hands with Idrees. They put him into the front seat of the Mercedes.

Once the vehicles began to move, Idrees slid down the window and shouted to Rab Nawaz.

"Oh, Rab Nawaz! Do me a favour, buddy. Take Dr. Manzoor from the clinic to my house and let him check Usman. He's not well."

"Don't worry, I'll take care of it." He waved at Idrees.

The two cars drove off, dust flying. Rab Nawaz inhaled his cigarette for a long minute, and then went to fetch Dr. Manzoor, letting out smoke that trailed behind him in the air.

* * *

Reaching Idrees' home, Dr. Manzoor checked Usman thoroughly and turned to Bakhtawar.

"Has Usman been afraid of fire since birth?"

"No, doctor *sahib*." Bakhtawar began. "I never saw that. Last year, he lit a lot of firecrackers on *shab-e barat.* When I cook bread on the stove, he's never scared or anything. But last night, when the man was burned, he was standing there and watching. Ever since then, this keeps happening."

As Bakhtawar was about to go on, the doctor stopped her.

"Oh, yes. I heard about that incident at the roundabout. Somebody was burnt alive last evening. Usman was also there? Well…most likely it's all because of that. Could be a hysteria attack. It will take some time, but he'll forget it. Keep giving him these," He pulled out some medication from his bag. "He will be all right in a few days. If he does not improve, bring him to the clinic. I will give him an injection now that will make him feel better."

He looked at Usman.

Usman started crying hysterically again and hid himself behind Bakhtawar.

"No, my child. Don't say no, please. My good boy, right? Take this one shot."

But Usman just cried more.. "Fire! Fire! Momma, fire! Fire!" He began to jump up on the bed and slap at his clothes as if he was aflame.

"Get hold of the boy, Rab Nawaz."

Usman jolted his hand out of his mother's grasp, pushed the doctor out of the way and dashed through the main door onto the street.

Rab Nawaz and Bakhtawar ran after the boy, but within a second, he ran back to the roundabout and hid behind the same broken wall at the end of the lane, putting his head down between his knees, trembling like a frightened kitten.

Chapter 5

Time: 10 am
Date: November 7, 2016
Location: Kabul, Afghanistan

Wahidi entered the restaurant and found a table where he could sit and wait for Nazir's call. He picked up a newspaper and looked through it. He found his own article and started reading. Once he was finished, he asked for a cup of tea, frustrated that he hadn't received a call from Nazir yet.

He decided to call Naimatullah Khan, a fellow professor at the university. Naimatullah didn't pick up. Just as Wahidi was going to call another professor, he finally received a call from Nazir Azizi.

"Where are you, Nazir? I've called you several times since the morning. What's happening at the university? You never updated me." His voice was full of frustration.

"Actually, I was in a situation there. It wasn't anything to do with the university. It was your article that was published in the Afghanistan Times this morning. A few student unions were protesting against that article and, as you know, there are some teachers behind all of these actions, trying to ignite a flame against you. I'm reading the article now, actually, and I see why everyone is so frustrated. You have written about national and religious ideologies, calling them 'artificial schools of thought, which are there to get political and economic benefit. If it weren't for this commercial use for such ideas, they would have been lost from the pages of history long ago.'

"Perhaps it's because you have written such heavy words here…'The concept of religionism and nationalism has turned the human world into an artificially commercialized, barbaric world, while on the other side, the animal world is absolutely natural.'"

"Oh, yes! What's wrong with that? Nazir, this isn't a new article," Wahidi emphasized. "It was published three months ago in the Washington Post before it was published in the Afghanistan Times. There, no one said a word about my ideas."

In a glum tone, Wahidi continued. "When will these people grow up? I don't know if they'll mature at all. Their tempers only get shorter with time…"

"I don't know either, but you should understand that this is Kabul. That's Washington. Do one thing. Don't go home. I've heard that there are some extremist militant organizations behind all of this. You know your past well, Wahidi. There's a chance of an attack at your house."

Nazir Azizi paused. "Why don't you come to my place and let this storm blow over? Just for a few days."

Wahidi was irritated. "What is this nonsense? Where have we been born? We can't write openly, can't talk freely…"

"Well, being born with these people…that's fine. Dying by them would be mere stupidity. I'm going home, as there are no more classes. Just come straight to my house. I'm calling my wife to make your favourite, lamb kebabs and bolani."

"As you say. I'll come over now." Wahidi put his phone into his pocket and pulled his car out of the restaurant parking lot and onto the highway.

* * *

Two hours later, Wahidi was having lunch at Nazir's place. They were still chatting about Wahidi's article.

Wahidi, in his usual pedantic tone, was saying, "Religion and nationalism are both attached to human needs, and get their strength from economics and money. Up to an individual level, it's okay. But once it goes to a collective level, it gets complex. When religion and nationalism enter the commercial market, negative consequences develop on both collective and individual levels.

"If we look into the evolution of human civilization, we will find that there are lines back to tribal culture. It starts with an individual, which turns into a family. Next, it becomes a neighbourhood, which forms a community, and then the entire village. All of these are stuck together, with artificial glues named religion and nationalism…am I not right?" Wahidi asked.

"But that's just the word people don't like. Artificial."

Putting some lamb kebab on Wahidi's plate, Nazir said, "They assume that you're neither Afghan nor Muslim. You're actually an infidel, agent of the enemy. That's why you criticize nationalism. You have no love for your own country."

Wahidi interrupted him with a raise of his hand. "No. It's not that simple. They're not children. Actually, they behave like this so people will start hating us. It's all politics for money. They don't want any modern thoughts that can lower their income. So far, the best sauce in the market is religion and nationalism, so who's going to close up shop? There's always a period to sell something. A market, too. One time people were entertained by record players. Then there were CD players. But nowadays, they listen to MP3s."

"Okay, I agree with you, but don't forget that we're from a country where free thinking and speech are not allowed. These people can hurt you, my friend. Why don't you understand?"

Wahidi sipped from a glass of water. "This is the time of internationalism. Today's people are citizens of a global world, where people who belong to different languages, races, religions, traditions and colours live together. The only strong tie uniting them is economy. We are not too far from a time when all of Europe was killing each other in the name of religion and nationalism during World War 2. Germany was bombing Poland and France was bombing the Germans. But now, they have been united as a family, have removed their borders, and are visiting each other without visas. So, where has all of this bloodthirsty nationalism gone? Where has so much love come from? Only economics. Nothing else." Wahidi finished his lunch.

"I accept your point on nationalism, but why must you also bring in religion?" Nazir Azizi gestured to some sweets on a plate, offering them to Wahidi. "It will simply cause bloodshed. Once a Molvi hears your views on the concept of religion being artificial, he will draw a conclusion from your thoughts. You're denying the existence of God, and then it will be straight atheism, no?"

Wahidi looked at the sweets with a smile, and replied, "Here, let me start off with the dish of sweets, because this is the bitter part. You'll probably get the answers by asking a few questions.

"Why are churches getting emptier in the West, while mosques are becoming more crowded in the East?

"Why, in the West, are science and philosophy so popular, while in the East, there's absolutely no interest in them?

"If you do find philosophy or science in the East, then it would be in China or Japan, where traditional religion doesn't exist and philosophy isn't directly attached to religion. Religion ends where philosophy starts. Even if there is religion in China or Japan, it would be Buddhism, and those beliefs contain no traditional concept of God.

"India is the only place seeing a new light after the partition: secular philosophy. Meanwhile its leftover, Pakistan, is now firmly in the grip of traditional religion, either caused by itself or created by the superpowers for economic benefit…you can see the difference between them.

"Tell me. Is religion really a natural phenomenon? In that case why doesn't nature favour believers? Now, don't give me clichéd religious thoughts. The truth is, some parts of the world have evolved while others haven't. In some parts, religion leads society, while in others, it follows it.

"Where science and technology are trending, churches have been left empty, and people are growing wealthy. Where scientific thought has not been created, society is economically declining. My friend, the essence is economy. Nothing else.

"During the religious era, economy was attached to religion. The stronger ruled with a pundit, a molvi, a messenger or a Son of God behind the scenes. Now, the need for the religious leader is over. Science makes people strong and prosperous without religion. Who cares about faith in God? Your life depends on the slight movement of a finger on a trigger. We have missiles and bombs. The time of preaching is gone. This political sauce is only on sale for poor countries so their rulers can make money by fooling their masses. This is also an evolutionary process; after a few decades, the scientific world will make this market collapse,"

Nazir Azizi laughed. "You're saying that necessity is the mother of invention?"

"Yes, and economy is the father!" Wahidi replied, laughing as well. "He has many wives, and the most beautiful one is religion. The second wife is nationality, the third wife is language, and the fourth one is tradition. Now it's his choice which one he wants to bring to the market."

"Don't forget, some of his children are spoiled ones, so be wary," Nazir warned.

"I understand, my friend." said Wahidi. "Let's have a cup of tea and think about what to do next."

At that, the friends walked into the living room.

Chapter 6

Time: 12:30 am
Location: Mississauga, Canada
Date: November 7, 2016

A current of fear ran through Sania's body as the loud voice of her mother coming from her bedroom clashed with the soft opening of the door. She felt as if an angry cheetah was about to pounce on her.

But there wasn't only a cheetah. In fact, behind the cheetah there was a wild tiger—her father—trembling in anger, looking as if he was ready to pounce on her and eat her alive.

"Ask this shameless girl what the hell she was doing! Sitting in the Starbucks restaurant at this time of night." He stormed in behind her mother, glaring at Sania and pointing at the clock.

"Don't ask me!" Her mother, hair mussed, also glared at her, frustration in her red eyes. She fell into a recliner and buried her face in her hands.

"Disgusting! Is there to limit to indecency? She'll get herself a beating, and I will give it to her! Get her out of my sight!" Her dad bellowed.

Her mom shouted, "Didn't you feel any shame, having a date with that Sikh boy! What *was* that shamefulness?"

Sania could not ever have imagined that such a beautiful, romantic date could end in such a horrible way.

She gazed at the floor. "Mama, his name is Daleep. He goes to my university and both of us are good friends." After a short silence, she jerked her head up. "We love each other."

"Shut up, you damned girl! You'll burn in hellfire!" Her mother screamed. "I would never have dreamt that I would have such a shameless daughter!"

Her dad struck his palm to his forehead in rage. "First of all, meeting a boy before marriage is a big sin, *and* on top of that, with one who isn't even Muslim! And on top of *that*, in a restaurant?! In front of everyone?" He spat, "Shameless! Why don't daughters like this just die as they're born? I used to preach to *others* about this, and today, my *own daughter* is indulging in such sinful acts."

Yelling in frustration, he turned to her mother. "Nelofer, Ask her! Did we send her to university for an education, or for a romantic affair? God…if our *own* daughters lie to us, then who should we trust?"

"Who *should* we trust?" Her mother repeated. "That's enough. We should just get her married. Look for a good Ahmadi family and send her off. And if you can't find a good proposal here, then let's go back to Pakistan. She's had enough 'education.' That's it. University is over, from today."

Sania saw her academic future disappearing.

"You're right. There's no need for her to go to university. Stay at home, Sania. There's too much drama in a university education!"

Oh, sit at home. Just what mother wants to hear. Sania thought with her heart, but didn't speak because she knew that one word would lead them to kill her.

Dejected, she slowly walked towards the staircase, but froze when she heard the voice of her mother.

"Where are you going? We're not finished. How long has this been going on for?"

Sania, her back to her mother, said, "Two years."

"So you were cheating on us for two years?"

"Mom, I wasn't cheating at all." She turned to face them. "You never asked me. I never told you. I knew you would react just like this!"

Sania's eyes began to water and her voice trembled. "Just because he's a Sikh, and I'm an Ahmadi-Muslim. I know that you're fixed on marrying me into an Ahmadi family. You've been repeating this to me as I grew, that we have a tradition of arranged marriages. If I had told you that the boy I love is a Sikh, would you forgive me? You would do the same thing you're doing right now. Mom, we haven't done any sin. Yes, we meet each other. Because we love each other."

Sania spilled all of this in one breath. She moved her gaze to the floor.

"So, what are your plans now?" Mama asked.

"Mom, I don't know what you want to hear and what you don't want to hear. Why I love a guy, or why I love a *Sikh guy*? Or why I didn't tell you all of this before? Why I kept meeting him in secret? All of these questions have the same answer. I didn't love him because he was Sikh, or a Muslim, Punjabi, or an Indian. In fact, I love him because he's a great human being."

As Sania spoke her tone gained confidence, recovering from her parents' attack. "And then, about *loving someone*? You also loved Dad. That's why you married him!"

"Shut up!" Her father roared. "There's no need to *justify* your shameful act. We were both Ahmadi-Muslims and both sides of our families made the marriage with utmost respect and honour to each other. We never met before marriage like shameless people do, and I spoke to your mother only after we were married. But forget all this. You won't understand. Now, listen to my decision. From now on, none of this is happening ever again."

He turned to her mother. "You don't need to ask Sania any more questions. I don't want to get into it any more. It is over. Now, let's do something for her marriage as soon as possible."

He turned back to Sania and snapped, "Go to your room, now! There'll be no talk on this subject anymore!"

Her father spoke with finality as if he just ripped out a tree and packed the dirt flat again. He stared at the floor.

Sania looked at her parents, tears in her eyes. She swallowed, then ran upstairs quietly and shut the door.

It seemed like the thud of the door gave a voice to Sania's feelings. All of her anger, pain, and frustration ran into the walls, which soothed her inside for a while, but rejected her from this home for life.

She sat on the bed and looked at the walls, thinking. Then she took out her phone and dialled Daleep's number. It was busy, so she recorded a message.

"Daleep, please call me back. I have a very important matter to discuss."

She got up from the bed and sat down before her computer, her gaze on the screen, half-hearted.

Chapter 7

Time: 10 pm
Date: November 7, 2016
Location: Shah Faisal Colony, Karachi, Pakistan

Hearing a knock, Bakhtawar opened the door of her house, expecting Idrees. Instead, she found Molvi Salimullah standing with a few bearded men.

Bakhtawar immediately covered her head and stepped behind the door.

"Oh…*Assalamualaikum.* Idrees isn't home." She greeted, her tone respectful. "He left for the mosque this morning. He's not back yet, though."

"Yes, yes, sister. We know that. We met him this morning. We wanted to tell you about something. May we come in?" Molvi Salimullah cleared his throat.

Bakhtawar stepped out of the way and said, "Oh, please. Come in." Two men walked into the house with him; he instructed the rest to stay outside. They sat down in worn lawn chairs scattered about the veranda.

Bakhtawar stepped towards the kitchen, covering her face with a *dupatta.*

She spoke anxiously, without using Idrees' name. "Is everything alright, Molvi sahib?"

The molvi replied, "Yesterday, some respected people from our community were infuriated by an infidel showing deep sacrilege to Prophet Muhammad. He was taught a lesson and beaten. He ended up dying, burning himself to Hell. Now, the police are going into their usual routine, investigations and everything. Brother Idrees' name is also in the list, amongst those the FIR reported."

He added, without looking at Bakhtawar, "Idrees is in police custody right now, but don't you worry, we'll get him out. It may take one or two days." He stroked his beard and looked at the floor. "We just thought to let you know. The police have taken in nine or ten other people along with him, but our mosque and the *Madrassa* is behind all of them. With God's will, *Inshallah*, we won't let one man stay inside. Everyone will come home with full respect. *Jazāk-Allāh*, all these brothers, including Idrees *bhai*, are doing a very righteous task for the honour of our Prophet Muhammad. A senior molvi, Shamsul-Haq, you may know him, specially advised me to deliver this particular message to you. You don't have to worry about him at all. We will support not only him, but all of them in these hard times and take care of everything.."

"But, Molvi sahib, will they beat him? I've heard that they thrash prisoners mercilessly at police stations." Bakhtawar wondered, panicky.

"Not at all, sister. They won't dare do that! Idrees has not committed any unethical act. He hasn't stolen or robbed anyone. Nor has he committed fraud with anyone. It's not a sin to send a blasphemer to his ultimate destination. The Quran strongly suggests keeping respect for the Prophet Muhammad and protection of his name mandatory for all Muslims. Brother Idrees has done a very noble deed. He has risked his life to send an infidel to hell.

"Sister, love of our Prophet is a blessing for a Muslim. He can take anything but disrespect to Prophet Muhammad. That Muslim wouldn't be even worth being called a Muslim, Sister, that does nothing after hearing disrespect for his Prophet. Our Quran has instructed us to respond harshly to those who insult the Prophet. History is a witness; Muslim Caliphs and

Sharia always beheaded blasphemers. Sister, nobody will dare touch him in the police station. You have my word. Idrees is a *ghazi*, a warrior for Islam. When such incidents happen, worldly laws fly away. Don't be worried. Just let us know if you need any goods or groceries - Rice, *daal*, *roti*…don't hesitate."

"Thank you, Molvi sahib," Bakhtawar sighed in relief. A thought occurred to her, and offered, "Molvi sahib, at least have tea or something to eat before you go."

"Thank you, sister, but we have to visit other sisters' and brothers' homes who are also worried. Such a bad time for us Muslims…people are being troubled after doing good deeds… may God have mercy on us."

Molvi Sahib and his associates rose and left the room.

Bakhtawar locked the door. Suddenly, she thought of something. *Oh, no. I forgot about where or how I could meet Idrees.*

She opened the door again and looked around. However, it was still dark outside and the only thing she could see was a pack of dogs chasing each other. Bakhtawar decided that she would call Rab Nawaz in the morning and ask about Idrees. She was locking the door again when she heard Usman crying. She crossed the veranda to her son's room.

Usman had probably been through another bad dream. When she came in, he was staring at the wall. As soon as he saw his mother enter his room, he moaned as if he was going to puke again. Usman's bed already smelled bad because of previous vomit. This had been happening since the morning. It had only stopped when he slept, around the time the molvi had come. After sleeping, he would start vomiting again every two minutes. He had thrown up the medicine prescribed by the doctor. Bakhtawar had not changed the sheet on purpose, knowing it would be spoiled again in a matter of time.

Bakhtawar brought Usman close to her and began to soothe him.

"What is wrong, my child? Were you scared again? Are you vomiting? Wait, I'll go get you something." But before she could bring back anything, Usman belched loudly, jolted forward, and vomited.

It wasn't a large amount since he had eaten nothing since morning. He doubled over with pain. Bakhtawar began to massage his back, slowly reading verses from the holy Quran and blowing on him, trying to ease his pain religiously.

Usman just looked at her face with sick eyes, holding his stomach and crying out for his mother repeatedly.

"You'll get well soon, my son." She cleaned his mouth with the dirty sheet and held him in her arms.

"I will get you medicine. Should I get you milk, too, my son?" She continued to stroke his hair with her fingers.

Usman, his face sick, said, "No, Mom. I will not eat anything. It makes me want to vomit."

Bakhtawar said to him, "Your father will be coming soon and I will ask him to get mangoes. Don't you like mangoes?"

Usman began to scream. "No, mama, no. Don't call Daddy! He's scary. No, mama, don't call Dad. No, no!" A small vomiting followed a big belch, and he began to scream again.

Chapter 8

Time: 12:00 Noon
Date: November 7, 2016
Location: Kabul, Afghanistan

The phone was ringing when Wahidi opened the door and entered his home. He picked up the receiver and an unknown voice spoke to him.

"Professor, we know everything about you. Where you live, what you do, and where you came from just now. This is your first and last call. After this it will be our bullet and your head. It would be better for you to stop writing all of that shit. You're a traitor, an agent of the Jews. You should know what we do to people like you. Don't take this call lightly. We've had complaints before, and we've kept an eye on you since then.."

"Who the hell are you?" Wahidi's face was red with anger.

"Taliban." The line disconnected.

"Hello…? Hello?" Wahidi shouted repeatedly into the phone. There was no response.

He put the phone back in its cradle.

This wasn't the first call. He had received calls like this before, but this time the tone was different. Wahidi looked at the phone for a bit and then sighed. He took out some clothes from his wardrobe and went to the bathroom to change. He came out wearing pyjamas. He picked out a book from a stack dispersed all over his desk and began to look through it.

He soon realized that he was unable to focus on the book. The phone call had created an anxiety that was crawling under his skin.

After a few minutes he got up and plugged in his computer. He logged into Facebook. He just felt like talking to someone without any reason. His mind was unfocused. Then he received a message from Sania in his chat-box.

"How are you, sir?"

"I'm okay. How about you, Sania?" he typed.

"Sir...do you have some spare time? I want to talk to you for a bit."

"Oh, sure. Go ahead."

"Sir, is love possible without taking colour, race, nationality or religion into account?"

"Yes..." Wahidi typed, and then thought for a brief moment, writing, *"If you consider colour, nationality, race or religion, all you get is hatred."*

In response, Sania typed, *"People who make relationships only when all of these ingredients are present...what would you say about that?"*

He typed one word in reply. *"Compromise."*

"An entire life can be lived with a compromise?"

"It's possible, but that life will be devoid of any real love."

"But, what would that life be like? It would be full of hatred, suffocation, anger, pain and tears..." Sania's reply seemed to be filled with emotion.

In reply, he wrote, *"Patience, and then habit."*

After sending this, he started to type again.

"Sometimes, by living together for a while, the two individuals start to like a few habits of each other, and people wrongly take it as love. If such a relationship is broken due to practical reasons, then both of them don't really feel much pain. Rather, they forget about each other quite quickly and go back to their daily chores. That way, it's pretty easy to figure out that the relationship was not based on love. It was a compromise."

Wahidi waited for Sania's reply, but she didn't answer for a few minutes. Wahidi felt that Sania was probably thinking before writing a message, as he could make out that something was being typed and then erased a couple of times.

Finally, a message from Sania came through.

"When every religion starts with love, and if the end is also love, then...why is religion divided so much?"

Wahidi replied, *"It's really the same for everyone, but it has been expressed by different minds from different eras. Followers of those minds absorbed it according to their era. But collectively, love was the central idea. It is a separate argument whether this concept is natural or unnatural, social or political, human or supernatural, and thus, it has become split into pieces after being divided by the different nations. This religious concept was used for political purposes because it attracted billions of followers. That's when the whole idea of religion was polluted."*

"Sir, how did religion originate?"

Immediately, Wahidi replied. *"From fear, ignorance and loneliness."*

"And love?" It seemed like Sania was surprised.

"Yes, religious intellectuals used love for the treatment of fear and loneliness. Due to ignorance, they created the concept of 'God,' and connected the above concepts with it. Thus, God, for psychological reasons, was divided and multiplied accordingly."

Wahidi was writing without any pause as if his eyes were closed.

"How you are so confident in your thoughts?" Sania asked with amazement.

Wahidi replied, *"Because 'God' was only created in religious places or eras. His survival wasn't possible where science and philosophy were established."*

"Sir, do you believe in love?" Sania typed reluctantly.

"Yes," Wahidi typed with all confidence.

"And you don't believe in God?" Sania typed faster this time.

"Not at all," Wahidi replied.

Sania thought before typing, *"Is love possible without believing in God?"*

"Yes, it's possible."

Then Wahidi followed this with another message.

"Actually, that's what real love is. Love that is developed without fear or loneliness. Thus, the relationship between God and love is actually questionable."

"Sir, can I ask a personal question? Have you ever loved someone?" Sania asked, reluctant again.

"Yes, but it has only remained as an ache." Wahidi replied with emotion. *"It has been twenty years since my love died. Now, I've moved on from the freshness of new love. The remaining ache is my strength and my support for living."* Wahidi typed, his thoughts flowing.

Sania asked, *"You never married again?"*

Wahidi typed, *"I couldn't marry my love in the first place. She was punished because she loved me."* Wahidi continued. *"She was accused of having a loose character because we met secretly. Her family killed her. They killed my parents, too. They also injured me seriously, but I survived. Now, her love is enough to keep me alive. After that, nobody could invoke the same feeling of love in me."*

"...was she of a different faith?"

"Yes. She was of a different sect. A different tribe."

Then Wahidi typed the last line. *"I don't believe in religion. And marrying anybody without love is an ethical crime for me."*

Wahidi waited for a response, but it seemed that Sania had nothing to add.

"Goodbye," he typed. He then turned off the computer.

Chapter 9

Time: 2:30 am
Date: November 7, 2016
Location: Mississauga, Canada

Sania's phone vibrated, and she picked it up and answered it. The caller was Daleep. She spilled everything in one breath. "See, Daleep? What we were expecting has just occurred. Everything's all messy now. Mom and Dad have found out. They saw us together at Starbucks. Now they're threatening that they won't let me go to university anymore."

Daleep took a long, deep breath. "Well…that's no good."

"What'll happen now?" Sania said, depression in her voice.

"I think we should give this situation a break and silently observe where everything goes. What you think?" Daleep said this slowly.

"Mom and dad have gone mad. Don't you understand?" Sania spoke in a weeping tone. "Your getup became a problem, and dating with a Sikh, not even a Muslim. I told you. My parents are traditional. They're very conservative."

"It's all right. Don't worry. We were already expecting no good. I know my parents will go crazy, too. They are also like that. Let's see what happens."

"What would happen? I'm not expecting anything good." Sania's voice rose.

"You know what? Don't worry. I'll do something about it." Daleep said quietly.

"What something are you going to do? Are we going to elope? Is this a scene from a Bollywood movie? You know what? They're talking about getting me married already. Things like that." Sania replied.

"You know, this isn't India or Pakistan. It's not that simple here. They can't just marry you off when they want to. Have courage. Nothing will happen unless we want it to. Try to understand. Let's see how my parents will react. The only difference is that I have to tell them myself. My father'll probably be okay, but Be ji will kill me."

After a pause he continued. "Don't worry. I'll make a call to India today. Let me convince my dad first. If he reacts negatively, then we'll see. Maybe my parents will say the same thing yours did. 'I sent you there for academics, and you are romancing.'"

Daleep reassured, doubted and planned all of this in a breath.

Sania mumbled, "At least your parents aren't here. I have to live here with mine and bear their anger and shouting."

"Yes, but I'm an Indian citizen, and you're Canadian. One day, my student visa is going to be over. Ultimately, I'll have to see my parents' faces, too."

"Daleep..." Sania, after a reluctant pause, asked, "...do you really love me?"

"No! We're enemies." Daleep joked.

Then he became serious. "How do I prove it to you, now tell me?"

Sania remained silent for a while, and then slowly replied.

"No...I just wondered. That's why I asked." There was a short pause.

Suddenly a sharp knock shook the door, and Sania's train of thought was disrupted.

"Daleep, there's someone at the door. I'll talk to you later."

Sania pressed the button, ending the call.

Her mother was at the door. Her face was strained, and her eyes showing deep pain and disappointment. Or perhaps Sania saw that because she was feeling the same way.

"Give me your cell. Your father wants it." She extended an open palm.

"Mom…do you think this is fair?"

Mom retorted, "I don't know. Don't talk to me."

Sania grumbled, "Why are you guys behaving so traditional?"

Mom replied, "Yes. We behave like that. We are traditional people. Just give me your cell phone." Sania turned, picked up her cell phone, and placed in into her mother's hand.

"What is the password?" Her mother asked.

"Daleep," Sania replied.

"His name is Daleep?" Mom glared at Sania.

"Yes."

"…if you're feeling hungry, come down to the kitchen. The food's on the table." Her mother spoke to Sania as if she was doing a great favor.

Sania snapped, "No, no. I'm not hungry."

When her mother left, Sania shut the door with a bang, falling onto the bed.

For a few seconds, she just stared at the ceiling for a while, before getting up and beginning to type up an e-mail to Daleep on her computer.

Chapter 10

Time: 8:00 pm
Date: November 8, 2016
Place: Shah Faisal Colony, Karachi, Pakistan

The night Shah Faisal Colony's police station was attacked, the entire area echoed with the sounds of people chanting. *"Allah-Hu Akbar!"*

First, Molvi Salimullah had come to the office of the Superintendent of Police, backed by four or five people. But when the discussion turned into a loud argument, constable Rahim-Daad turned to the SP and whispered, "Sir ji, these people have come prepared. Outside, men are equipped with not only sticks, but with guns too."

As he heard this, the colour of the Superintendent's face changed, but he controlled himself and asked in the same tone. "How many people do you think are out there?"

"Around two to three hundred."

The superintendent turned to the molvi. "Okay, okay, Molvi Sahib. Please relax."

But Molvi Shams-Ul Haq warned the SP harshly. "There are only two hundred today. There could be two thousand tomorrow. This is a matter of blasphemy. Not an ordinary event."

"Look, Molvi Sahib, please…we just wrote some dummy First Investigation Reports against unnamed people. After all, we need to keep someone in the cells for that murder. Try to understand, Sir ji. We have to answer our superiors."

Molvi Shams-Ul Haq nodded. "There are a few of your superiors that we also know. We understand your legal restrictions, so we'll tell you this in friendship. Throw in a few drunkards instead. After all, they're burdens on our society. When are they going to be of any useful purpose? Let these good people go. They're people of the mosque…good Muslims. To be honest, the Quran and the *Hadith* encourage killing blasphemers."

Was it the inflamed speech of Molvi Shams-Ul Haq, or the effects of the two hundred armed believers outside? Or the sleeping beliefs of the superintendent himself, which were awakened by the holy speech of Molvi Shams-Ul Haq? For any of those reasons, he immediately made several phone calls, establishing the gravity of the situation with people who should know. Then he ordered constable Rahim-Dad to release the prisoners listed by Molvi Salimullah.

* * *

When Idrees returned home from the police station, he was pleasantly surprised to see the entire neighborhood in front of his house, a feeling of happiness in the air.

His wife was especially thrilled, distributing sweets among the crowd.

After some time the crowd faded away, and Molvi Salimullah came to him and whispered, "Idrees, tomorrow after the *Isha Prayer*, Molvi Shams-Ul Haq is coming to my home for dinner. He especially wants to see you."

Idrees bowed, put his hands onto his chest in the traditional gesture and promised he would come.

Slowly everyone left except for Idrees and Bakhtawar, who were standing in the doorway waving the guests away.

When they came into the bedroom, Usman was in a deep slumber. Idrees and Bakhtawar walked out and sat in a *charpai* placed in the veranda. He gave a long yawn and lay down.

"Bakhtawar, I'm tired after the long day, today. Tomorrow morning I have to go to the Mosque for Fajr. Molvi Sahib reminded me to never miss a prayer anymore and give more time to the Mosque."

"Oh, that's good." Bakhtawar responded with a smile.

"Now listen, Bakhtawar." Idrees took out a bundle of rupees from a pocket in his pyjamas and placed it into her hand. "Keep these inside the cupboard."

He took off a garland and tossed it onto the floor. He then turned over, facing his wife, and smiled.

"So much money!" Bakhtawar's eyes sparkled. "Where did you get it all?"

"Oh, that's nothing. Molvi Salimullah gave it to me. He has told me to leave the odd-job business and start working only for the mosque. He also said to keep an eye on the people near or far from the neighborhood so that they don't use any abusive words about the Prophet or his companions. Molvi Shams-Ul Haq, Molvi Salimullah's superior, would like to meet me after the *Isha prayer*s. He wants to discuss my responsibilities for the mosque. This is all holy work, and the good thing is that I'll be paid well. What else do we need?" Idrees said, looking into Bakhtawar's twinkling eyes.

Bakhtawar held the money in her hands and looked up into the sky. She said pleasantly, "That's why they say, 'There is always light behind the darkness.'"

"Thank God. Looks like my going behind bars was lucky for us." Idrees grinned at Bakhtawar.

Suddenly he remembered something. "Oy, how's Usman doing? Is he still puking? I'd asked Rab Nawaz before leaving to take him to the doctor. Did he do that?"

"Oh, yes," she replied in the same tone as Idrees. "Dr. Manzoor came and checked him and gave him some medicine, but he still throws up sometimes. Doctor sahib told me that the boy was really scared after seeing that man burned on the square. He was shocked by it. It'll take some time to get better."

After a few seconds she said, "Wash your hands and face. I'll bring some food for you." She began to walk towards the kitchen.

"No, no. I'm not hungry. I've eaten a lot of sweets already." Idrees yawned. "I'm going to sleep. Turn off the light. I have to wake up early tomorrow." He turned over to the other side of the *charpai*.

After entering the room, Bakhtawar cautiously opened the door to cupboard to put the money inside. She felt that someone was watching her from behind.

She turned around in fear, but there was nobody there.

Outside, Idrees was peacefully snoring. Inside, Usman was also sleeping, but a tear shone on his cheek in the light spilling into his room.

Chapter 11

Time: 12:30 pm
Date: November 7, 2016
Location: Kabul, Afghanistan

Wahidi turned off the computer and took a deep breath. He got up from his desk and sat down in a recliner, his hands resting at the back of his neck. He was feeling depressed after his discussion with Sania. The wound in his heart had begun to ooze again after a long time.

The memories sank into his heart, drop by drop. Time was pushing him back into his past.

Wahidi let his eyes close and felt that his tears, instead of wetting his cheeks, were seeping deep into the dark well of his heart.

A voice echoed from his subconscious, quivered and made itself heard. "The real war starts after the war."

Professor Zamanullah was talking to his graduation class.

Wahidi found himself twenty years ago, watching a young Wahidi raising his hand and asking his professor a question in Pushto.

"So, do you think the war will *ever* end, sir?"

The professor turned to Wahidi, but didn't say anything.

* * *

It had been seven years since the war with the Soviet Union started.

While the fumes of war had spread all over Afghanistan, the major battles were taking place in the mountainous provinces. Life was still running in the capital city of Kabul.

Occasional bomb blasts echoed in the city, but the electricity and water mains were still working. Markets were open. The Kabul University's classes had been minimal, so Wahidi borrowed textbooks from the library and studied at his friend Sherazi's home.

Sherazi was Wahidi's paternal cousin and classmate. He was also a good friend of Masood, Sofia's brother.

Sofia, Wahidi's love at first sight.

October 16, 1985, late evening. That was when he saw Sofia for the first time.

He remembered that day. Dozens of soldiers from the Red Army were marching through main market of Kabul, weapons strapped to their backs, returning to the Soviet Union.

Suddenly, Wahidi was thrown back by a massive blast. Huge clouds of smoke filled the area, buildings and shops collapsing amidst the fog.

Sherazi was sprawled on a corner of the street. Wahidi grabbed his arm, and both of them hurried to seek shelter. Running across the market lanes, they found themselves in front of Masood's home.

Masood opened the door, and Wahidi saw Sofia standing behind him.

That moment. All the time in the universe had stopped just for them. It was a moment where their hearts pulsated only for each other. It was a moment where he opened the windows of his heart for a girl he would love for all his life.

The love of his life was standing right in front of him. Sofia had completely numbed his mind at that moment, but he could remember her now. Her deep, hazel eyes had imprisoned the beating of his heart. The light falling onto her face had brought unique colours into his soul. Her smile, the flutter of her eyelids, the few strands of hair falling onto her face and the way she pushed her hair behind her ear and looked at him with innocence in her eyes.

God, was I living that day, or had I found my nirvana?

When Masood had opened the door and asked them to come into the living room, Sofia quickly disappeared into the home. Then Wahidi saw the mortars, Kalashnikovs and hand grenades scattered throughout the room. He had never seen such a large collection of weapons in such a small place.

That was the day Wahidi found out that Masood was deeply connected with *Gulbuddin Hekmatyar*, leader of the *Hezb-e Islami* political group, which was responsible for the blast Wahidi and Sherazi had just escaped.

The next time Wahidi saw her, she was standing at the desk of the Kabul University library, signing out some books. When he looked at her, she smiled and gave a friendly wave.

They walked together in the corridors, chatting about their studies. She was studying fine arts and was now in her first semester. Her brother was not happy with her going to university, but her parents were supporting her. She was surprised to know that Wahidi was from Bamiyan, and was staying in Kabul only so he could get a bachelor's degree in political science.

"You look different from when I saw you the first time," Wahidi said slowly. "Russian jeans and an Afghani scarf look better on you."

"Yeah, I've noticed that Kabul culture has been changing quickly,"
She replied with a smile. "We're changing from jeans and shirts back to
Shalwars and *Burqas*. You don't have a beard, but most of the boys do,
now."

"You're right," Wahidi said. "Soviet and Western dressing are now
being taken as *kufr*. Unfortunately, the propaganda from the Mujahideen
has turned the Afghan-Soviet war to a Believer-Infidel war. Extremism is
all over, and Soviet culture is slowly disappearing."

Sofia didn't reply. She looked at the ground as they stopped in front
of a classroom.

Wahidi turned. "Sofia, I'd like to see you again."

Sofia gave a slight smile and walked into the classroom.

Wahidi's heart was wandering in the streets of the past, and his
present was being coloured with images of Sofia. He didn't know when
his eyes closed, or when he fell into a deep sleep.

As waves of wandering thoughts filled his mind, he was taken from
Sofia's beautiful eyes to the devilish, cold faces of the Taliban.

He found himself in a night where many politicians were sitting
around the dining table, speaking loudly about the war between the Soviet
Army and the Afghani Mujahideen.

"It has been the blessing of the *jihad* and the efforts of the
Mujahideen. We are achieving success in the war!" Masood's voice
echoed throughout the room.

"No," Wahidi raised his finger. "It isn't a war between Islam and
kufr, but rather between communism and capitalism."

Masood turned to Wahidi. "These living room orators don't know the basic concepts of ji*had*!" He pointed towards the ceiling. "Allah has promised to protect His followers Himself, just like He sent the *Ababeel* birds to protect His home, the *Kaaba*. He has motivated other nations to help us fight against the *Kufr*."

Wahidi watched himself give Masood an amused smile. "Where were these *Ababeels* when the Prophet's family was ruthlessly murdered in *Karbala*?"

The silence that followed broke Wahidi's dream.

Wahidi was shaken out of a daze by the piercing noise of glass shattering. He got up from the recliner and scanned the room, not finding anything. He walked out onto the balcony, looking around.

He heard the faint noise of a gun firing, and suddenly light and pain flashed through his forehead, and a rush of blood flooded down his face.

He hit the ground, falling into unconsciousness.

Chapter 12

Time: 12:00 Noon
Date: November 7, 2016
Location: University of Toronto, Canada

Daleep and Sania had been sitting in the university compound holding hands for the past two hours. Sania looked very worried, while Daleep was deep thought. After being silent for a while, he sighed and looked around the compound.

All over, students of both genders were sitting in groups around tables or standing nearby, either immersed in their studies or chatting.

There were Indians, Pakistanis, Bangladeshis, Chinese, Africans, Canadians and Europeans. All of their faces were bright and alive.

Faces were conversing, and so were eyes. Voices were echoing, and so were smiles.

There were no feelings of difference amongst race, colour, or religion. Neither height, build, nor appearance.

But yes, if there was anything, there was a link between everyone. A link of love and friendship above all of these prejudices.

Despite November, the weather wasn't extreme yet, and the ground was still covered with verdant grass. Autumn was revealing a mosaic of colours on the trees, shining red, green and yellow. The leaves were turning from green to a shade of pink as if autumn was at the peak of its vitality. Instead of reflecting sadness, all was immersed in a unique feeling of joy.

The wind felt cool, but still seemed warm as the bright colours of the sunny morning were absorbed into it, giving off a tender taste of winter.

Daleep regarded Sania with a deep gaze and then slowly grasped her hand, wishing they could be part of the global society around them.

"So…how did you come out of the house?" he asked.

"I put sandals on," Sania mumbled, and then started to laugh. "Daleep, you're too much."

She sighed deeply. "What did I write to you in the email last night? That I wanted to meet you and make a decision. Mom and Dad can't understand what's happening. They're still mentally living in Pakistan!

"In fact, they've never lived in Canada. Not for a day, a night, an hour, or even a minute. They don't know anything about this country, about its culture, its colour. I don't think they even know the name of the tree that has grown in their back yard for the last ten years! What's the name of that bush? Near the bedroom window?

"And you know what? They don't care. They just moved here to make dollars. They immigrated here for big cars and beautiful houses. They don't even care about the social system of this country, the new civilization that's being developed here, what the past was, and what the future is going to be. They don't care. Only thing they care about is their visits to Pakistan twice a year, and to Europe three times a year, so they can post their pictures on Facebook to make their friends jealous and show off to their relatives in Pakistan. They love going back to Pakistan to tell relatives what their kids are doing in Canada. 'They're geniuses. They're always the first in their grade. They've become doctors…they've become CEOs of a company…and our house is on the most expensive road in Toronto, and we have two BMWs now…'

"They try to find their happiness in all of this rubbish, but I'm not like them. I hate all of that. This is my country, Canada. I love its culture, its language, because this is what I am. I'm Canadian; that's it. And I want to live here, in this country. I will live my life here because this is what my home is. This is what my culture is. I'm like these people," Sania gestured to the students nearby. "I don't want any Pakistan in my life anymore. Nor its culture. I don't want to go back. Because I know the people over there are all hypocrites.

"They lie without any reason. Not even for benefit. They don't want to listen to the truth, be it from themselves or from others. They're after each other's lives, like savages. They live in hatred. I can see through the news, through society, through our family and friends. And I can't afford all of this nonsense. Daleep, listen. I've decided that we have to do something with our lives. We have to inform our parents about our decisions, instead of asking them about their decisions."

Daleep replied, smiling. "That's all right, but you never told me how you got out of your house. Did you jump the wall or over the gate?"

Sania giggled. "Am I really a Bollywood heroine? My dad had gone to work and mom was sitting in the basement, watching Pakistani morning TV shows. I put on sandals, plugged in my earpods and headed straight to my Daleep. I thought, 'I better go before her useless show finishes and she decides to come upstairs and scold me!' I'm sure she must've called Dad half a dozen times." Sania looked at her wristwatch.

"Why don't you move to my place?" Daleep smiled.

"Yeah, so I deliver at least three babies before I even marry, and you fly back to India after getting your Doctors' degree. And me, I become a psychopath instead of a psychiatrist after raising three children as a single mother.

"No, Daleep. We have to come to a serious decision today." Sania smiled and held his hands in hers. "I was thinking last night. Look, if I go back home, Mom and Dad might even beat me out of anger, or marry me off through flattery. It's very easy to find someone for this kind of arranged marriage. There is always some aunt who's dying to see the flowers around her son's neck bloom. And their sons are dying to come to Canada through these social marriages. Everyone likes buying one and getting two. I don't want all that garbage in my life. Period.

"I'm not going back home. And maybe I won't live with you either. But I am thinking about moving in with a friend. You know me, Daleep. If you marry me, I'll live with you. And if it's not possible, I've thought that through, too. I'm still not going home, but yes, I'll review our relationship further. I think I'm being fair, and I'm making the right decision."

"Sania…don't you trust me? Do you think I just flirt with you?" Daleep had been hurt by her words. "You don't need to go anywhere else. And please, don't feel like I'm going to run away and leave you in the middle of nowhere. Listen, you can leave me, but I'll never leave you. I already know my dad will agree to the marriage…but Bi ji…? She'll never accept it. So there's only one way left. I'll hang around and ignore her decision, and ultimately she'll change it. It could be possible that I have to shift to Canada permanently, because India and Pakistan both have a close family system. Since you're here, I must leave the idea of going back to India. I hadn't even thought it through to this point, but I'm beginning to think that we have to start deciding."

Daleep took a deep breath. "Sania, I love my Bi ji, my mom, very much. Like the way you love your parents, despite what's happening. But don't worry, please. There must be something better in our future. Just trust me."

Perhaps Sania had wanted to hear all of this from Daleep. She gazed into his eyes. "I trust you more than myself, Daleep. That's why I left my home, my parents and everything just for you. Whatever you think, it wasn't easy for me."

Daleep embraced her. "No, of course it wasn't easy, Sania, and I will live with you until my last breath."

They stayed that way, feeling the comfort of each other's presence for some time. Daleep felt as if Sania was emotionally filled. She had started to cry silently. Daleep could have felt those tears on his neck, in his chest, and then in his heart, without looking at her eyes.

He held Sania more tightly and murmured into her ear. "I love you with all my heart, Sania. You are my love."

He felt that his words went down into Sania's breaths and became part of her heartbeat, as he felt the same beat in his own heart.

Their love was slowly growing indifferent to culture, colour, religion or race.

Daleep and Sania's merging completed the disconnected scene of the university compound. Nature was getting involved in making them part of the same global society, where the things from outside were different, but the inside was the same.

Chapter 13

Time: 2:00 pm
Date: November 7, 2016
Location: Kabul, Afghanistan

As Wahidi gained consciousness, he was struck with a painful headache. He was still lying on the floor of the veranda where he had fallen after the bullet hit him. There was a pool of dried blood on the floor where he had fallen. He was worried that his eye had been hit, because the flow of blood from his right eyebrow had clotted, making it impossible to see.

Wahidi got up painfully and wobbled back into his room. He felt for the doorknob and locked the door. He stumbled into the bathroom and looked in the mirror. Relief washed over him. It was only blood from his eyebrow; the eye wasn't damaged.

He washed his eye and all of his forehead, cleaning away the clotted blood, and then looked into the mirror at the tear in his eyebrow. It was mostly dry, but the corners were bleeding a little. He took his first-aid box from the cupboard, cleaned his wound and placed a bandage over it. Then he took two tablets of Paracetamol.

Back in the living room, he peeked out of the corner of the window. As he expected, he couldn't see anyone nearby. *It started with verbal abuse, and now they have started shooting. It looks like my mouth isn't the only thing they want to silence.*

Wahidi took out his cellphone and dialled Nazir Azizi's number.

After Nazir heard about what happened, his voice sounded frightened. "Wahidi, don't even think about leaving your house until I show up with a couple of friends. Listen, grab a handgun and keep your door locked."

When Nazir disconnected, Wahidi put his phone away. He sat down on his bed and closed his eyes.

In just a moment, his cluttered thoughts slowly brought him into the past, gathering themselves into the shape of Sofia.

Sofia embraced his mind in the form of a rainbow emerging from wandering waves, filling his heart with love and affection. He was just about to lose himself in her romantic colours when the devilish faces, cruel beards and cold gazes of the Taliban appeared, instantly filling his heart with a nausea of hatred. The visage of Sofia's brother, Masood, stood out among these faces. Wahidi saw his red eyes blaze with hatred, and the guns in his arms flicker with flames, burning holes in Wahidi's chest, sinking him in blood.

He felt that his life had been split between the first thirty years and the second twenty. The first thirty years he had experienced his dreams, hopes, desires and loves. Then the next twenty years took over: guilt, frustration, depression, pain and battle.

The first thirty were the years of his childhood, his youth…full of the love from Sofia, his parents and his younger brother, who had all been snatched away from him.

My enemies have guns, bullets and hatred. I have paper, pens, and love. My words are stronger than their ammunition.

Wahidi took a deep breath, pulled open his bedside drawer and took out a handgun. He made sure it was loaded and then set it close by. He noticed his book when he was closing the drawer.

Civil War in Afghanistan. Published in 2001. A smile spread across Wahidi's face, and he remembered himself trying to convince people that the civil wars of 1996 and 2001 were basically extensions of the war that originated in 1978.

What a mess, Wahidi put a hand to the wound on his head.

Where have the superpowers' evil interest brought us? First it was the Russians, then the Americans. First the Republic of Afghanistan, and then the Islamic State of Afghanistan.

He shrugged and looked up at the ceiling.

He put the book back into his drawer next to another one of his books: *From the Death of Shah Ahmad Masood to the Death of Osama Bin Laden.*

The destiny of political Islamization, Wahidi thought before closing the drawer.

Wahidi remembered how they had come to this point.

*Ugh…a lot of innocent people have given their lives without knowing about how economics has utilized religion for political reason under the pseudo title of ji*had.

Who should we blame for this? America and Russia, who fought each other in a rat race between socialism and capitalism? Or Pakistan and Saudi Arabia, who fought each other, one greedy for money, and the other wanting to spread Wahhabism? Or the Taliban, al-Qaeda, the Islamic movement of Uzbekistan, and the Northern Alliances, who fought each other in the name of sectarianism, racism and nationalism?

Who should we blame for this?

The thoughts were coming and going, and he was thinking about how he had come to this point in his life.

He remembered the article he wrote a few years ago on the Taliban's abuse of women. It had been the front-page story in the Kabul Times and had also found a place on international media. That's when he started to get the threatening calls—when he wrote articles blaming the Taliban for the rape and killing of civilians.

That was when TV news started showing his article, and the Taliban committed a suicide bombing that caused the deaths of five journalists.

Wahidi had been warned by a staff officer of Kabul University security forces to be careful. He had been a pain in the neck for the Taliban, which is why he had been getting so many threatening phone calls, not to mention the bullets.

This train of thought was broken when the doorbell rang. Nazir Azizi and some students had arrived to pick him up.

Chapter 14

Time: 9 pm
Date: November 8, 2016
Location: Shah Faisal Colony, Karachi, Pakistan
Idrees' next day was spent entirely in the mosque.

From his *Fajr* prayer in the morning to his *Isha prayer* in the night, there was a line of people standing to congratulate him. Whenever people came to the mosque and saw him, they would approach him immediately so that they could shake his hand in respect.

Some people would bow their heads, and some people would kiss his hands. All of this was a very pleasant change in surroundings for Idrees. He had never been through an experience such as this before.

"Assalamualaikum, Idrees!"

Idrees turned, and found his neighbor Salahuddin, who owned a convenience store nearby.

"How are you, Idrees *bhai*? Surprised to see you in the mosque at *fajr* time."

"Oh, it's all Molvi Salimullah's blessing. He offered me the right path of life, and I felt that I had to be there. Other than that, what have I done in my life? I would've been just another sinner."

"Oh, no, Idrees *bhai*. I know you. You're a very good person. You always help out others in our community. I remember you helped me out when my car was broken…and you helped Jamil Khan's son when he fell into a gutter. You collected donations from all over to seal the holes so that it would never happen again.”

“Oh, that’s nothing. You would’ve done the same if my son Usman fell into the gutter.”

“But now you’re leading the community, after doing such a brave deed. I heard some guy was using bad language for Muhammad.”

“I think there are a lot of educated people in our community. Doctors, engineers, lawyers…how am I a leader?”

“No, Idrees *bhai*. A high education isn’t necessary to become a leader. A leader should be courageous and religious, like you are now. You should be the counsellor of the community.”

“Oh, no, Salahuddin *bhai*. What you’re saying is just because you like me. Otherwise, you know…I haven’t even passed 8th grade.”

“Allah-Hu Akbar! Allah-Hu Akbar!”

They heard the sound of someone chanting the Azan on a loudspeaker, and it was Molvi Salimullah’s voice, which Idrees recognized immediately.

“We should go inside. The prayers are starting.”

As they turned around to start walking, Advocate Mohammed Wakil ran up to Idrees in the mosque, and not only kissed his hand but also kissed his forehead in admiration.

Idrees felt pleased and respected by this sudden event and Salahuddin nodded wisely.

Idrees had a Tasbī in his hand, and he was mumbling a verse from the Quran, also keeping a scarf around his neck like Molvi Salimullah. While Idrees was praying, his mind was on the conversation with

Salahuddin, and the respect from Advocate Mohammed Wakil. Everything that had happened in the past three days was rolling through his head like a film, making him feel like an honourable and reputable man.

When the prayers had ended, his ego was at its highest. The inflation of his religious narcissism was in an infantile stage, but the roots were spreading rapidly. The holy environment of the mosque, the purity of the atmosphere and the respect from the community had been developing a junior Molvi Salimullah inside of him.

Time passed so quickly that he never noticed when Isha was over. The entire day had passed in praying, reading the Quran and meeting with others in the mosque. After the day's prayers, Molvi Salimullah walked over to him and whispered in his ear.

"I just got a call from Molvi Shamsul-Haq. He's on his way to my house in half an hour. As I said before, he wants to see you there."

Idrees looked around and whispered back. "Are others coming for the dinner, too?"

"No, brother. This dinner is only for the important people. Let's move. I have to get some milk and desserts for the dinner. Brother Shams likes cold *Lassi* and warm *Gajar-Ka-Halwa* sweets."

This was the first time Idrees would meet Molvi Shamsul-Haq. However, he had heard much about him. His short statements were usually published in the back pages of the newspaper, in which he always focused on initiating the *Sharia law* in Pakistan, and always spoke in favor of the *Daesh*'s Islam and against the Shia and Ahmadi's *Kufr*.

Idrees didn't know what political or religious party Molvi Shamsul-Haq belonged to, but he was impressed by his power and popularity. He knew that he controlled a lot of mosques and *madrassas* throughout the country, and he had appointed people like Molvi Salimullah to run every mosque.

Fifteen minutes after Idrees and Molvi Salimullah reached the latter's home, a long line of expensive cars drove up and parked in front of his gate. Molvi Shamsul-Haq and his three companions were in one big car, with armed, bearded men in the cars behind. They didn't come out of the car and stayed outside.

Molvi Shamsul-Haq's companions had beards spread over their chests. Two of the four were Molvi Shamsul-Haq's relatives, his son and brother.

When Molvi Shamsul-Haq saw Idrees, he exclaimed a verse from the Quran, *Sūrat Al-Tawbah*, and when Idrees moved forward and kissed both of his hands, the molvi replied by holding his shoulders and kissing Idrees' forehead.

After a pause, he said, "Well done, Idrees. The only punishment for a blasphemer is death. The protection of Prophet Muhammad's honour is mandatory to every true Muslim. You have raised our heads in pride. An infidel had enough courage to dishonour our Messenger?"

Idrees had developed confidence from Molvi Salimullah. Despite this, he decided to ask Molvi Shamsul-Haq directly. "Molvi sahib, do you think we're going to get any problems in the future from the law and the police?"

"You think these infidels have the courage to do anything against you? Why are we here? There would be a storm from here to Islamabad, Idrees *miyan*. Don't you worry. Listen, this was the responsibility of the state that you have taken. That's the only thing. What you did was the responsibility of every Muslim for the honour of Islam, and for its establishment. But we'll talk about it. Let's go inside and start eating. Eh, Molvi Salimullah sahib? Let's have dinner."

"Of course, come in."

Saying this, Molvi Salimullah looked around and invited everyone inside. He led Idrees by one hand and scratched his beard with the other. He brought him into the dining room where he arranged many plates of food and drinks. There was a colorful cloth in the center of the carpet, with pillows around the room.

There were also beautiful hand-embroidered flowers on the corners of the cloth and the pillow covers, and also flowerpots at all four corners. There was a spit-pot for tobacco and *paan* in one corner.

The smell of *agarbatti* wafted around the room, giving off fumes and making the same environment as in a *mazar*. On one wall hung a large painting of the Masjid-e-Nabvi, while there was a picture of the *Kaaba* on another wall. Both pictures were decorated with golden frames.

In the center of the Dastarkhān the steaming food was spreading an appetizing smell of grilled chicken, tasty *biriyani*, spicy *korma* and delicious *seekh kebabs*.

After Molvi Shamsul-Haq sat down, each of his companions also took his place to start eating.

Molvi Shamsul-Haq personally asked Idrees to sit near him and then started filling his plate with *biryani* and *seekh kebab*. He said, "*Bismillah*, Idrees *miyan*. Let's enjoy the food."

For some time the noises of spoons and plates echoed throughout the room. Gradually, a conversation started.

Molvi Shamsul-Haq addressed his host, "Yes, Salimullah. What was that Station House Officer saying?"

"Well, he was telling me how the situation was getting hot. For a few days, Human Rights and Civil Society Pakistan will raise this incident, getting propaganda on the media and the newspapers. They'll be trying to attract business through this advertising, but soon everything will calm down."

Molvi Salimullah offered around a plate of *naan*. "Molvi sahib, I said the same thing you advised me to say. Many drug addicts are wandering around the community. Arrest them and keep them behind bars, instead of our honourable people. Molvi sahib, you're a hundred percent right. I also hinted that Molvi Shamsul-Haq has friends in high places. And about the sticks? I told him to keep in mind that if he wants to play with sticks, we also have lots of brothers who are ready to fight back."

After saying this, Molvi Salimullah placed some roasted chicken on everyone's plate, insisting for them to have more. He insisted, "Brothers, please do justice to the chicken. You're being hesitant."

Molvi Shamsul-Haq burped and then raised his hand. "Oh no, Salim sahib. Look, brother. There is no pressure in our religion. Don't say things that will cause conflict. We're against bloodshed. Our Islam is the religion of peace. There are a few people who don't understand that there are laws in *Sharia*. These *Sharia* laws are all from *Allah Tabarak'Tallah*. Are we not going to follow his orders, *nauzubillah*? Now, as for the blasphemy incident, there is no room for discussion, dialog, or arguments, because to defend respect of Muhammad, we can take someone's life and give our own life too.

That SHO is also our man. He just has to show the hard collars of his uniform at the police station. And you know what? There are always some spies from the newspapers around the cells too, and we don't know who has connections with whom. We need to proceed in a very cautious way."

After saying this, he turned to Idrees. "Okay, Idrees miyan. You have some important tasks. Number one is to fill out the consent form for our religious party, so you can be an official member of it. You will get a lot of benefit from this, because our party takes care of our members like their own children. Number two, since you're doing your religious duty, why not have your *sunnat* too, by growing your beard longer than your fist. "

Molvi Shamsul-Haq smiled, touching the hairs on Idrees' chin.

He continued, "From now on, give more time to the religious party and the mosque than to your painting job. Because in addition to our prayers, we need to teach and spread Islam to more people, especially when the Muslim *ummah* is distracted and a victim of ethical deterioration. It's the *farz* of a Muslim to propagate Islam, teach the values of our religion and try to bring them back to the straight line, *Seerat-e Mustaqeem.*"

"You're right, Molvi sahib." Saying these words, Idrees felt joy in his chest. Life suddenly became so kind and such a blessing to him. On the other side, he had a surprising thought confusing him.

Why, suddenly, is everything going into my favor? I am beginning to see that everything happening to me is coming from Allah.

Otherwise, how come I'm getting attention from such high religious leaders? And how come I'm being showered with money and respect? I'm just a handyman, and all of this respect? I'm sure Allah created me for a special reason. Molvi Shamsul-Haq was right, as he said that for honour and pride in Islam, we can sacrifice our lives, as our lives were given by Him.

Molvi Salimullah took a chicken leg out of the pot and placed it on Idrees' plate. The spoon clattered off the plate, abruptly breaking Idrees' train of thought. He looked at the spoon, picked it up, and put it back onto his plate.

Chapter 15

Date: November 13, 2016
Location: Toronto, Canada

Many days had passed since Sania had moved into Daleep's house. Her parents had called her several times. The anger and frustration at the start of the calls had slowly turned into begging, requests and promises. They had tried everything to convince her; moral and ethical values, family traditions, culture, reputation, respect, social and religious aspects and consequences. They had given her long lectures about the differences of Eastern and Western family systems as well as the religious differences between her and Daleep. She was reminded of all of their sacrifices and efforts throughout her growing up.

When there was no effect, they threatened her that they would stop seeing her face for the rest of their lives; she would be thrown out of their family.

But Sania didn't change a bit.

* * *

"Aren't you surprised?"

Sania's father, sitting in the living room, shook his head. "I am. What kind of magic has this Daleep used on our smart, beautiful Sania? She can't understand the consequences of her actions!"

Sania's mother replied from the kitchen. "Do you think this is because of a lack in our upbringing? She's never been like this before. It's all from her university, don't you think?" She looked at her husband.

"Yes, you're right. I had never really been convinced about co-education at any level. Especially in universities, where young girls and boys get along freely and start odd relationships." He took a deep breath and continued. "Sania always wore a *hijab* because of the Islamic school we arranged, but once she entered university, she tossed it away! I still can't forget her words when I asked her to put it back on."

"What did she say?" Sania's mother asked.

"She said the *hijab* wasn't related to religion and instead is related to Arabic culture."

"Was she right?"

"I don't know. Maybe or maybe not. I never really thought about it. But what I do think is that the *hijab* gives a woman modesty."

"What was her problem? Did she not feel the same way? Was it because of her rebellious nature…or did she have an authentic reason?"

Sania's father shook his head again. "You know what has always been cooking in her mind. She said something…the *hijab* had never been a religious necessity, and it's connected with Arabic culture. It was always there, ever since Arabic women wrapped cloth over their faces to protect themselves from dust and hot wind."

"Oh, where's she getting all of this from? Did she really discuss all of that with you?"

"Sometimes. Don't you remember when we were driving to Chicago, and she was talking so much about all that history and philosophy? The customs of veils…remember she insisted on taking it off when she started university?”

“Oh yes, I remember. But I told myself she was just growing up, and in a few years she would be mature enough to understand the difference between Western culture and our culture. I never knew she was so serious about it.”

“No, she was serious. In curiosity, I read one of her e-mails to an Indian friend of hers when her inbox was left open and she was out of the house. At that time I was wondering about whether she had any relationships, but I found about all of this, and it’s still in my drawer. Let me get it.

Sania’s father brought a sheet from his bedroom.

“So this is what I found in her e-mail, and I was kind of surprised,” said Sania’s father. “I think she was trying to convince her friend to get rid of a *hijab*…

“…the religions born in Arabia adopted Arabic culture at the time. Similarly, those religions born in India, like Hinduism and Buddhism, adopted Indian culture into their religion. That’s why they didn’t put any restrictions, like *hijabs*, on their women. You know what? Catholic Christians and Jewish women also wear *hijabs*. This dress started even before the birth of the Abrahamic religions. If we read human history before religion, the time of Judaism, Christianity, or even Islam…even then, Arab women wrapped cloth over their faces to protect themselves from dust and hot wind. But in Canada, people don’t like staring at each other, and there isn’t any dust or hot wind. We’re girls from the 21st century, and shouldn’t be living the 14th. We both know how girls come in wearing *hijabs* and then hide them in lockers once they reach university. I hate that nonsense. For God’s sake, let’s live normal lives like the others. I want to seem decent because of my education and my profession, not because of my appearance.”

After reading, Sania's father put his glasses down and looked at his wife. "See this?"

He put the paper on the table in front of Sania's mother, who said, "You didn't say anything to her after reading through all this?"

"No. First of all, she doesn't know I read that e-mail. She might not like it. Secondly, I'm a father, too. I had another thought, which I've never really spoken to you about. But, you know…she's going to get married sooner or later, and we would like to have good proposals for her. The *hijab* itself might become an issue as it hides the face. I'm sure that was the real reason we both let her go to university without a *hijab*. You know—even though we didn't openly talk about it."

"You're right. She was a good student, though. Where did this Daleep come from?" Sania's mother frowned.

"That was a shock for me, too, and I did some research when she left home. I found this e-mail when she talked to someone…maybe a university counsellor." Sania's father started reading another e-mail:

"I was willing to do a Masters in Philosophy, but gradually my interest has turned to psychology. I think philosophy has given me enough intellect and maturity to develop an interest in analyzing society above the level of traditional concepts. To be honest, my collective social views have now begun to affect the regular activities of my life, and to understand them I think studying psychology will be necessary. A change in my activities means I have started criticizing my own role in society. I've begun to refuse the concepts of my life that were generated on the sole basis of traditional and hereditary values. Please consider my serious interest…"

"I see," Sania's mother nodded, but it was obvious she didn't really understand. "Anyway, what about Daleep? How did he come into her life?"

He started flipping through more pages of e-mails that he had printed out.

As the sound of the pages echoed throughout the room, her parents thoughts' vibrated along the echo and faded into the past, learning about how Daleep and Sania fell in love.

* * *

"Well, you are completely different from me. See your appearance?" She pointed to his turban. "You're Sikh, and I'm Muslim. You're a Punjabi-speaking Indian, and I'm an Urdu-speaking Pakistani. Your culture is totally different from ours. Your clothing, too, sort of…"

As Sania paused, Daleep laughed in his loud Punjabi style. "Sania *ji*, every philosophy in the world starts with love. If there was no love in the world, there would be no human beings. If there were no human beings, what's the point of religion, culture, colour, customs or values? The first men to love in the world; were they Ahmadi Muslims, or the Sikh followers of Guru Nanak? Were they Urdu-speaking Pakistanis, or were they Punjabi-speaking Hindustanis? No. They were only humans."

And then, showing both of his dancing thumbs to her, he spoke with another laugh. "…or maybe only animals!"

Sania looked around, but nobody in the cafeteria noticed his loud voice except for her. She loved his carefree style of talking. He was so natural that even with effort she could not find any artificiality in his approach. Sania felt that Daleep's heart and his tongue were connected to each other. Whatever thoughts had originated in his heart would immediately come onto his lips in the same form.

After listening to all of these simple words from Daleep, she had lost her philosophy, psychology and heart to him. She decided she would need an honest, simple friend like Daleep for her whole life.

72

Sania's father took a deep breath and tossed the papers into a corner. He mumbled to his wife, "You remember, Nilofer? Sania's stubbornness grew as we pressured her. She was so irritated, don't you think? That's when she told us, 'If I ever marry, I'll only marry Daleep.'"

"Yes, I know. It was like she had just dropped a bomb onto our heads."

"I still feel that it was our fault, raising questions about her character. She was frustrated and felt as if we were criticizing her for living unmarried with someone."

He pulled out another sheet from the stack. "Let me show you another e-mail."

"I don't know who this guy is…Wahidi. Is he a professor? An online friend of hers? Whoever he is, she wrote some serious questions here."

"Professor Wahidi, sir: I have developed strong doubt about the feminine character of religion. I have asked myself several times why a woman's character is connected to her genitalia? How could a woman's body be her friend and her enemy at the same time? Why has a woman's strength turned into her weakness? Why is sex deeply seeded in the roots of religion? Why was the entire social structure of ethics pillared on its artificial basis? Why did religion use the support of lies to promote a truth? Because on one side, it talks against racism. On the other side, to promote itself, it restricts interracial marriages. If I am Muslim and he's Sikh, why were religious and social pillars shaken by our union? Why can't my future kids be half-Muslim and half-Sikh? And why can't we follow two religions at the same time, because God, or *parmatma,* is only one for everyone?"

* * *

While Sania's father was reading, Sania sat in her apartment room, confused, frustrated and anxious, thinking about why Professor Wahidi was absent online.

"Why did Professor Wahidi stop signing into Facebook?"

Sania was living in Daleep's two-bedroom apartment in downtown Toronto. It was still difficult for her parents to believe that they both loved each other but they were living like good friends, meaning they weren't sharing a bed together. But that was the truth. They wanted to make sure that their love was not from their sexual attraction but for the similarities of their personalities. Each of them considered the other's presence necessary.

That's why when one of Sania's close friends teased her, asking if Daleep was going to be a common-law partner.

Sania replied quickly, "No, I'm not."

"Why not? When your parents don't give you permission, and you guys are attracted to each other, then live together. What's the problem?"

"Even if Daleep and I have some differences, there are many things we have in common."

"Like..?"

"Well, we are both dreamers of the future, and both of us have agreed to create ourselves through academic growth. That's why I think we both have the same mechanical and spiritual approach to life. That may have been the reason we are seeing our love in mature eyes as adults and trying to understand it in the same vision."

"Oh, gosh." Her friend took her hand to her forehead. "How deep do you guys think about this?"

"Why not? After all, this is a matter of our love, which should be above the general, social, and religious values. You know what? We've had discussions with each other on almost a daily basis on this topic, but are unfortunately still unable to come to a conclusion for how a hindrance was created in our hereditary shape with the artificial or natural social bindings, causing difficulties in creating a new world for us."

One day Sania mentioned her Facebook friend, Professor Wahidi, to Daleep. She told him how Professor Wahidi was not only a political intellectual, but also had deep insight into the evolutionary process of human psychology, which had a role in sociology and economy.

When Daleep heard about Professor Wahidi, he was also interested, which led him to try a Google.

"Hey, Sania. Here's your Professor Wahidi. He's a smart guy. See, he's a professor in Kabul University, Afghanistan. He teaches international relations and political sciences. Look, he's written so many books. Here's his blog and a list of articles."

Daleep pulled up the facts about Wahidi one by one on his screen.

"Hm. So this is Professor Wahidi. That's why he sounded so impassioned and mature in his conversations. I already have a lot of respect for him. And now I have more because he's never introduced me to all this." This thought brought Sania to the biggest question of her life.

"Which concepts in our life are natural, and which are constructs from society?"

The answer to this question would be the answer to her love life, too

Chapter 16

Date: November 14, 2016
Location: Shah Faisal Colony Karachi

Within days, a beard had become a prominent part of Idrees' face. On his head, all the time, perched a white mosque cap. The *Surma* in his eyes, pyjamas above his ankles, the long shirt with a wide hemline and the woven *tasbi* around his finger had made him feel a better Muslim than others. On the repeated advice of Molvi Salim, he had stopped using abusive words. He had also changed his tone to an artificially polite manner.

Something his friends didn't notice, but Bakhtawar did, was that he was using new phrases and words in conversation: "Allah is merciful," "It was given by Allah," "Allah is our overseer," "All of these are intentions of the *Rab-ul-Izzat*!"

Even when Rab Nawaz or Kallo asked him how everything was, he would reply by touching his chest in a humble way, putting his hands to his ears in an apologetic way, and looking towards the sky in a praying way. "Allah is merciful."

All of these actions had become a part of his conversations.

Perhaps all of this had come from training by Molvi Salimullah, or due to the constant company of Molvi Salimullah's followers.

He was now — voluntarily or involuntarily — adopting all of this into his attitude. Using words like *Masha'Allah*, *Subḥān-Allāh*, and *Alhamdulillah* created a sense of security deep inside of him. It also expanded his ego.

It was Molvi Shamsul-Haq who taught him that intentionally using a couple of memorized words from another language not only showed a special relationship with that language but also displayed an admiration for it.

"Don't use "thank you," "sorry," or "excuse me," anymore. This is *kafir* language. We have to use words like *Masha'Allah, Subḥān-Allāh,* and *Alhamdulillah* instead," Molvi Shamsul-Haq emphasized, in the same way Molvi Salimullah had asked him not to use abusive words.

They also tried to convince him not to feel inferior because of his lack of education. "People who have received a worldly education are, in fact, absolutely illiterate, Idrees."

"How?" he asked, surprised.

"Because they haven't been blessed with a religious education, and will not develop intellect or understanding about how Arabic is the most pure language in the world, as it is the mother tongue of Muhammad *Arabi.*"

They also taught him that, "The Quran was also blessed into the Arabic language, which meant that the noble language was a priority for *Allah Tabarak'Tallah.*"

They repeatedly said, "When a Muslim uses phrases from the Arabic language, he receives appreciation, *sawab,* from Allah. And naming Allah in Arabic would be a thousand times better than calling him *Khuda* in Persian."

This was all very new for Idrees when he heard it from Molvi Shamsul-Haq.

"Arabic food, dress, style and culture are superior to that of other nations because Muhammad, peace be upon him, was from the Arabic race."

That's how Idrees was taught that the Arabic nation was the best nation in the world.

For the last few days, Idrees had developed a sense of love for Arabs. It was Molvi Shamsul-Haq who also showed him the difference between the *Wahabi* and *Deobandi* sects of Islam.

Before all of this, he had thought all Muslims were the same, but Molvi Shamsul-Haq was the one who was kind enough to explain to him, in simple but sharp words, "*Shias* have always been enemies of Muhammad's companions, the *Sahaba-Ikram*, and they are the ones who damaged the unity and the religion of Allah. They are the real enemies of Islam. Even more than the Christian *kafir*."

Now he understood how bad the *Ahmadis* or *Qadiani* were.

"Idrees, if you are ever are confronted by a *Qadiani* and a snake, you should smash the head of the *Qadiani* first, because they will never trust the belief that Muhammad was the last messenger of God."

He now realized deeply that *Qadianis* were the biggest enemies of the core of Islam and had always backstabbed it.

There were many discussions like this. Idrees took in all of it, surprised. *Why have I wasted my time and never bothered to learn these things before?*

Before this, he hadn't even known about the sects his friends belonged to. Molvi Shamsul-Haq and Molvi Salimullah knew everything about everyone's sects. In private gatherings, they would call *Shias* and *Qadianis* dogs. Sometimes when they were in an angry mood, they would use abusive words for them—but they would avoid doing it in public.

One day, Idrees asked Bakhtawar to start wearing a *hijab* and always to use a veil in front of relatives and strangers. Bakhtawar took his word, since he had been changing himself, and after that she had started to wear a *hijab*. The changes in Idrees and Bakhtawar were noticed by his family, relatives and close friends.

Now, even his childhood friend Rab Nawaz had become a stranger for Bakhtawar. Before this, Rab Nawaz would walk into the house whenever he liked, and ask Bakhtawar for *roti* and water any time. Bakhtawar would also serve him like his own sister without a thought.

Now, he had also sensed changes in Idrees and become self-conscious.

Once, he was walked with Idrees to his home. When they reached the main door, Idrees left him outside, not even inviting him in.

When he came back, he had two cups of tea in his hands. They drank it together outside.

Rab Nawaz realized that it was intentional because Idrees was talking about the concept of *mahram* and *na-mahram*, something that Molvi Shamsul-Haq had taught him.

Now, Bakhtawar, who was like a sister for him before, had suddenly become *na-mahram*. After this, Rab Nawaz avoided going to their home alone. He would prefer to knock on the door when Idrees or his family were at home.

Idrees had asked Bakhtawar many times to send Usman into the *madrassa* so he could start learning the Quran. But Bakhtawar was reluctant, perhaps because Usman hadn't been acting the same after what happened at the roundabout. Before, Usman would usually be playing on the street with his friends and would enjoy flying kites. Now, instead of playing, he would sit in the corner of the house for hours, without any sleep.

Sometimes he would start up in the middle of the night when everyone was sleeping. He would begin to cry and scream…and then wake up later and hug his mother. Before, he would laugh loudly, but now, he didn't smile at all, especially when Idrees was home. Now, he would hide in his blanket all the time, or play with his toys in the corner.

"Idrees, have you noticed our Usman? He's been changing a lot."

"What changed?"

"Well, I've noticed that he cries and screams for the smallest things at one time, and then suddenly stops crying and reacting to anything the next, staying quiet for several hours. Is he okay?"

"I don't know, maybe something's wrong. I saw him several times sitting in the corner while his friends were playing on the other side. He was quietly watching people in the roundabout, counting the wandering animals or making tiny houses in the mud. I don't know why he's doing all this. We'll see," he reassured Bakhtawar.

Even after all of these changes, Bakhtawar wasn't unhappy. Idrees' income had increased by a lot. Sometimes he brought stacks of rupees and gave them to her to keep in the safe.

"Idrees, we need new furniture. We have enough money to do it. The walls have been repainted, and the ceiling is also fixed."

"Oh, why not? First, I'll install an air conditioner. It's too hot in here," He said with a smile.

Bakhtawar thought, "*Allah'miyan*, thanks a million. You ultimately brought fortune to our home. I stupidly felt as if it was a crisis when Idrees went to jail. I didn't know it was actually a blessing."

Chapter 17

Time: 11:00 pm
Date: November 14, 2016
Location: Kabul, Afghanistan

A couple of days at Nazir's house had freshened Wahidi up quite a bit. He had many visitors during his stay: not only chancellors and professors from the university, but many of his close friends, students, and journalists from all levels of media.

News of the murder attempt had spread quickly through electronic media from the local newspaper into the international press. A swarm of messages from friends piled up on Twitter and Facebook, even from people he had never met, but they all knew him because of his thoughts and writings. Whenever he found spare time, he made notes on many important questions he intended to write on in the future.

Nazir's house had become an interview studio. Talk show anchors would try to reach him for radio and TV interviews about this incident, and sometimes newspaper journalists visited, which made him feel optimistic about getting his message across.

One day, a popular journalist by the name of Jhanghir Khan, a man famous for his deliberate cross-questioning, came to Nazir's house and sat down for a detailed interview for the Afghanistan Times.

Once the technical equipment was set up, Khan started right away. "How has journalism been affected during this political change throughout the last three decades?"

Wahidi took a sip of tea, peacefully sitting in the living room. "The electronic and print media of Afghanistan was destroyed by the three decades of civil war after the Soviet Union's invasion. After the Taliban's rule ended, the media gained great freedom. As you remember, hundreds of magazines, radio stations, TV channels, and national-international news agencies started in business. But to get to that level, our own community had to pay. They had to go through not only physical but also financial hardship. They had been kept in darkness during the war so that the outside world could be kept innocent of the massacre in Afghanistan."

Mr. Khan raised a finger. "Where were the liberal thinkers like you at this time?"

"That's what I'm saying. The liberal thinkers who spoke against these policies were silenced, so the world wouldn't recognize the collective consciousness already created in Afghanistan.

"Back in that time, when Talibani forces were departing from Afghanistan, they were fighting the free media with a vengeance. They were constantly harassing secular thinkers, intellectuals and the press. People like me were writing articles on the social expectations developed from all of these political changes. That's how we've come gradually up to this point—and we're still fighting."

The journalist nodded. "How do you see these cultural conflicts in the global sense, nowadays?"

Wahidi replied softly, "The common people of the future Afghanistan and countries like it could develop a political, social, and economic consciousness. In my understanding, it isn't vertical, but horizontal, social differences that generate conflict in the global civilization. As a consequence, a new social order is developing."

Jhanghir Khan shook his head slowly. "Sir, what do you mean as 'vertical' and 'horizontal?' Do you mean the vertical society is a hierarchy, and the horizontal is more democratic, spreading to all people?"

Wahidi smiled. "Yes, but it isn't that simple. The vertical society is formed more through genetic descent. The original birthplace of many religions was the Middle East and South Asia - all Abrahamic religions, Hinduism, Sikhism and Buddhism. Horizontal is more the spread of culture. These religions were spread to the rest of the world, but the bondings of those followers are different."

"Because they are chosen intellectually, rather than instilled through centuries?" Jhanghir Khan asked.

"Exactly." Wahidi beamed on the reporter as if on a precocious student. "In the same way, tribal culture has its own values deeply connected to the original geography running through the genes of its believers vertically. That's why I used the word subconscious for vertical, and conscious for horizontal - A conscious phenomenon is a socio-political one, while an unconscious one is a religious one, the most difficult and the worst cause of conflict between cultures."

Wahidi sat forward earnestly. "Understanding doesn't happen in the vertical, but on the horizontal plane. Belonging in the vertical plane is an unconscious process, while the choice to participate in a horizontal plane is a very conscious one, and affected by social conflict. Its dimensions are directly connected to the political, cultural, economic and psychological roots of the society. This new social setup is developing, and at the same time affecting both planes of the world. I think the change in consciousness is directly connected to the intellectual evolution, the horizontal one."

"So is this cultural conflict a good or a bad thing?" Jhanghir Khan asked firmly.

"The clash of cultures could actually have a positive or negative affect on the next step towards the future. The societies fallen in love with the past could be seen basically as very strong structures standing on the pillars of religious basis.

"Their roots have been spread into the neurons of the brain in multiple layers. If the society of the future completely ignores those layers and tries to create a new shape that manipulates the clash of cultures for political purposes, then it may generate negative instead of positive results."

Jhanghir Khan was still not defeated. "But what about the general population of underdeveloped countries, that have little education or intellectual impulses?"

"These masses always remain in a world of gossip, rumours and baseless blame on the politics of the developed countries, so that they gain a temporary relief of mind, but stay in a permanent world of chaos without finding any real solution," he answered, shrugging with a smile.

"So…what's the verdict? How will this be resolved in the future?"

"I wasn't surprised when I found that secular people around me appreciated my thoughts, but at the same time they felt that the political and social conditions in Afghanistan have still not developed to a level where this sort of argument could be openly spoken. Again, I have a different point of view," Wahidi said.

"Any necessity has to follow the laws of nature. The darkness of illiteracy and the light of consciousness cannot walk together. A blind person cannot differentiate between the dark and the light. How can we expect that from a man who has no vision at all?"

Jhanghir Khan moved on. "What about the incident last year regarding your written article? I heard there was a commotion in the University of Kabul because of it."

Wahidi nodded. "Last year, my article on the generations of idolatry in Islam put my life in danger. For me, religion died through idolatry. Religion would never survive if there was no faith in idols. For example: Muslims kiss the name of Muhammad, or the Quran, or the stone placed in the Mecca during the haj, just like Hindus bow their heads in front of their scriptures.

"Each and every word of the Quran has become an idol. As Muslims, without knowledge of what the words even mean, we continue to follow the Quran. Even those that read the translation continue to look only at its superficial, linguistic meanings. They did the same thing with their religious personalities. They created an idol of their messenger of God, Muhammad, who destroyed 360 sculptures in the *Kaaba*. The destruction of the sculptures gives the impression that he was against idolatry. But his own followers have made him an idol.

"My article was written with a background of other Abrahamic religions like Christianity and Judaism, in comparison with non-Abrahamic religions like Hinduism, Buddhism and Jainism. It also discussed Aristotle's philosophical image of religion in extensive detail.

"There was a lot of debate on this article at the university, even by the professors. Soon, a political group had formed against me. The group felt that my writings might turn the university into a political-social wrestling ground." He said with a smile. "According to them, this kind of discussion would be premature for the time and could develop detrimental effects."

When the reporter had left, Nazir shared his opinion with Wahidi. "Maybe those professors were right, back then. Of course, their biased opinions were partly due to the jealousy coming from your popularity, but you have to consider the consequences in the form of physical and mental trauma to you, now. You're a smart man, Wahidi. I'm sure you'll come out from this challenge like you did in your past. But I still worry."

Wahidi kept a smile on his face. "Oh, really? You shouldn't worry, my friend."

Later in the evening he was reading some comments online and answering replies to his interviews published on Facebook and Twitter when he received a message from Sania, asking him for an opinion on some of her personal matters.

Wahidi replied, "Sure, Sania. Most welcome." But she did not respond. Perhaps it was too late, as she wasn't online anymore. Wahidi then also signed off and shut down his computer.

Chapter 18

Time: 1:45 am
Date: November 16. 2016
Location: Mississauga, Canada

Sania, not wanting to wake Daleep, left her bedroom silently, but was surprised to see that lights were on in the kitchen. Daleep was absorbed in a medical magazine, eating cookies with tea.

He turned his head to her, then brought his gaze back to the magazine. "Hey, didn't you get any sleep without me?"

"It's a quarter to two in the morning. If my *Dallip Kumar* is involved with some other *Saira Bano*, then that's what will happen." Sania smiled, referring to an iconic Bollywood couple.

Daleep shook The American Journal of Medicine in his hand and mumbled with a smile, "This *Saira Bano?*" He resumed his reading.

A thought crossed his mind. "But Sania, this Saira Bano does not give romantic heart attacks…she stops clinical heart attacks."

"Oh, let me see."

Sania took a bottle of water from the fridge and took a sip. Slowly, she started massaging his neck and shoulders. "Cardiac Resynchronization Therapy—Why, What, When, and Who." Looks like an interesting article."

"Yes," Daleep replied. "With signs of heart failure, if a patient's left ventricular ejection fraction is 35% or less and if the QRS complex is 120 milliseconds or less, then resynchronization therapy is very important."

"Really," Sania smiled and slid her hand from his shoulder to his heart.

Daleep smiled, took his hand from the packet of chips and laid it over hers. "Oh, in this situation, we'll need a defibrillator with the resynchronization, because in a sudden cardiac arrest, both of them would be protective."

Daleep tugged her hand, and Sania slipped from the arm of the chair onto his lap.

Daleep closed the magazine, put one hand on her shoulder and lifted her chin with the other hand, kissing her on lips.

Sania locked her fingers behind his neck and closed her eyes. They kissed for a long while, and then she embraced him tightly.

Daleep squeezed her with love and nuzzled her neck.

After a while, she opened her eyes and spoke softly, looking into his eyes. "Mamma called again."

"Oh? What did she say?" Daleep held her gaze.

"The same thing she always says. She says it is better to move somewhere else rather than live with you. She thinks that even if we don't have sex, people will think we are involved. So far, this news hasn't spread through our relatives, but if not today, then tomorrow everyone will know. Especially in the Ahmadi community, not only here in Canada but also in Pakistan. Then, consequences will not be good."

Daleep replied with a naughty smile, "Oh, if it's like that, then we should do it wholeheartedly. After all, if that's what people think…"

Sania looked into Daleep's eyes. "So you think we are not doing sex because of the people around? You think our love will not be complete without sex?"

Daleep laughed. "You know what? People take love and sex as one thing. They think genitalia and heart are driven from one embryological remnant."

Sania joined his laughter for a moment. After they stopped laughing, both of them looked at each other, and Sania said, "Why do people think so differently in this world?"

"What do you mean?"

"What if I am an Ahmadi Muslim, born in Karachi, Pakistan, and my family is non-Punjabi? What if you are a Sikh, born in East Punjab, India, and your family is Punjabi? Why do religion, nation, and race have to intrude into our love?"

Daleep took a strand of her hair from her cheek and put it back behind her ear. "Where? See, I've removed every hint!"

He kissed her on the lips again, and Sania closed her eyes. Both of them were lost in each other's love.

After a while, Sania opened her eyes and took a deep breath. "I wish everything was so easy. By the way, Daleep, did you get a chance to talk to your Abbaji and Beji?"

"Yes, and I hinted to dad that I like a girl but didn't say much about your background yet. I know he says everything to Beji. It'll be hard to hide."

"Daleep, what do you think? Should we really marry each other? Have you ever thought…once we have kids, what would they be? Ahmadi Muslims? Or Sikhs? Who will they marry? Ahmadi Muslims or Sikhs? What culture will they adopt, my people's, or yours? Will they talk in Urdu or Punjabi? Are they going to bow in front of Guru-Nanak or Musleh-Ma'ood?"

At first, Daleep was silent, meeting her gaze. Then his eyes sparkled with a sudden naughty thought. "Don't worry, we'll use condoms." He laughed loudly.

Sania slid from his lap and tried to grab him. Daleep jumped from his chair and started running around the table.

Sania, laughing, ran after him, but after a while she lay down on the sofa in the living room.

Daleep sat at the other end of the sofa, then took her feet in his lap and started to massage them.

Sania lay there for a while. Then she sat up. She got up and took her laptop from the table. She logged onto Facebook. Daleep saw her typing on the laptop and smiled. "Looks like tomorrow's weekend has already started tonight. Want me to get you tea? I also have to finish that article."

"Yeah, I'd love tea. Please."

Dallip bowed his head as a waiter does. "Yes, my darling." He walked into the kitchen. Sania realized that Wahidi was logged in on Facebook and started typing.

"Hello sir, how are you? I saw you were attacked…how are your wounds? Who were they?"

After a while, Wahidi's reply was on the screen.

"I'm completely fine, Sania. I'll tell you all about it. You had said that you needed to tell me something personal? Is everything okay?"

In reply, Sania's fingers began dance on the keyboard.

Chapter 19

Date: November 16, 2016
Location: Karachi, Pakistan

By the advice of Molvi Shamsul-Haq, Idrees had been devoting most of his time to *Madrassa-e-Deenyat*, a religious school connected with the mosque. There were over 200 students in this school, and as requested by Molvi Salimullah, he and Molvi Shamsul-Haq were teaching the Quran, Tafseer, Hadees and the Fiqah.

Idrees never saw Molvi Shamsul-Haq doing any teaching. Perhaps it was because he was busy in the administrative portion of the school. Instead, Molvi Salimullah had arranged Imams as their duty to provide education in the school, especially having the children memorizing the Quran and learning how to pray *namaz*.

For Idrees, the culture of the *Madrassa* was new; he had never been to one in his life. In fact, there had been no *Madrassa* in the neighborhood when he was a child. That's why his father had arranged for Molvi sahib in the mosque to teach Idrees the Quran.

One day, Molvi Salimullah took Idrees into an office in the *Madrassa* and told him all about its background, since he had heard the rumors from the media. He didn't want Idrees ever to be confused on this matter because Idrees was a man of spare literacy and intellect. He hadn't even known if Muhammad was born in Mecca or Medina, or where his tomb was located.

When Molvi Salimullah curiously asked him about the first *Kalima,* the first Declaration of Faith for Islam, he recited it perfectly, as he, like all Muslim children, had memorized it in his childhood.

"Yes, this is what we call the *kalma-e-tayyaba*," Molvi Salimullah said, smiling.

But when he asked about the second Declaration, Idrees had nothing to say, sitting there scratching his head.

But when Molvi Salimullah said the first few words.. "*Ashadu an la ilaha illa'llah...*" It sparked his memory, and he recited the rest: "*...Ashad anna Muhammadan Rasululu'llah.*"

He had heard this during his childhood and used to read it during his prayers. But, like most Muslims, he hadn't known its literal meaning, and that the Second Declaration was called the *kalma-e-shahadat*.

Molvi Shamsul-Haq had advised Molvi Salimullah to take special care of Idrees. "He is a brave Muslim with strong nerves, but he is very emotional."

Molvi Salimullah informed Idrees that in this *Madrassa-e-Deenyat*, most children were around 8 to 12 years old. Parents brought their kids in, not only for the religious education, but poor parents would find good shelter for their kids, with free food and drink.

There were many things that Idrees didn't know about the history of *Madrassas*. Like how the *Madrassa-e-Deenyat* was one of about 50,000 *deobandi maslak Madrassas* in Pakistan, which were built by General Muhammad Zia-ul-Haq to create young *jihadis* during the middle 1980s to defeat the Russian invaders in Afghanistan.

"Did you know, Idrees *bhai*, that there once were more than 500 students in each of our *Madrassas*. But Musharraf's government decreed bans on most of these *Madrassas*."

"Oh!" Idrees raised his brows in surprise and curiosity. "And then?"

"Well, our *Madrassas* had been registered by the efforts of Molvi Shamsul-Haq through the Pakistani *Madrassa* Educational Board. That's why they were never able to ban us completely. Okay, now tell me, Idrees. Do you know about the *Lashkar-e-Tayyaba* and *Jamat ud Dawa?*"

"I have heard rumours about them, but I never understood what they were really doing in Pakistan." He replied.

"This is very important to know, Idrees. Most of our people don't know, but these organizations are doing hard work to spread Wahhabism in Pakistan, because the pure soul of Islam is actually embodied by Wahhabism, practiced by the *Salafi* sect. It is connected with the holy residence of Muhammad—peace be upon him—Saudi Arabia, while other sects, particularly the *Barelvi* sect and the *Ahle Sunnat Wal Jama'at*, are full of impurities. They go to the tombs of saints and pray while Muhammad was against even keeping record of graves and tombs instead of making places of worship."

Seeing that Idrees was interested, Molvi Salimullah explained in detail. "*Qawwalis* and *Milad Sharifs* are all impurities and sins descended through Hindu culture into Islam while it was growing in India. There would be punishments in pure Islam for all of these."

Idrees changed the topic and asked about the use of *Madrassa-e-Deenyat* for poor children.

Molvi Salimullah replied, "In our *madrassa*, kids not only received religious education, but also meals three times a day. We have more than 50 rooms in the upper floors of the building. Four kids sleep in each room, and there are arrangements for everything, including kitchen, laundry, health, security and almost everything required for daily living, so it isn't a small administration to run.

"Brother, it is the only one example of hundreds of *Madrassas* in the city, and you will be surprised to see that they are all under the supervision of Molvi Shamsul-Haq."

* * *

One day Salimullah took Idrees to Molvi Shamsul-Haq's residence, which was located at the Defense Housing Society in Karachi.

"Oh, *Allah'Miyah*."

Idrees looked up at the size of the villa and his eyes widened. He had no words; he was just silently regarding the entire street where a line of security guards stood outside the building near a long row of Mercedes and Pajero jeeps in the parking lot.

He scratched his head, and Molvi Salimullah heard him mumble something softly. "Allah'Tabarak'Tallah has really blessed Molvi sahib. I'm sure he's doing what He wants. I wish I could devote myself like Molvi sahib."

Molvi Salimullah glanced at Idrees and found a strange spark in the man's eyes, but he couldn't understand the source. Was it from spirituality or materialism?

After this, Idrees always made very certain he was running the Madrassas' activities in a way to never damage Molvi Shamsul-Haq and Molvi Salimullah's confidence in him. Even though he was involved in the Madrassas' activities, his life was on track, which it hadn't been before.

Molvi Salimullah gave him special advice. "You should keep yourself to the Madrassa and never involve others, close friends, those in the neighborhood in these activities."

"What about my wife?"

"Especially your wife. For the last few years the government had been changing the policies against the Madrassas and has been causing trouble."

95

"That's terrible. What can we do?"

"Don't you worry. Molvi Shamsul-Haq is dealing with it all, very cautiously. These are dangerous times. You must understand the importance and delicacy of the job we are doing."

"Oh, I know how important this is."

"Politics in Pakistan rolls around like a prostitute changes her customers, and the interesting thing about her behaviour with her customers is how each man is always made to feel that he's the favourite one.

"This is the same Pakistan as it was originally. It had a total of 189 religious Madrassas. Thanks to one man, *Mard-e-Momin Mard-e-Haq*, or General Muhammad Zia-ul-Haq, this was expanded to 40,000 in 2008. It has been said that God creates his own ways, and this is what happened when the infidels of Russia attacked our neighbouring Muslim country, Afghanistan.

"Then the same Islam, which had only been official for the last 30 years, suddenly became reality and spread all over the country. Pakistan became the strongest fortress of Islam in the world. During this time, most of the Islamic countries, especially the Saudi Arabs and Middle Easterners, stepped forward to help their Afghani-Muslim brothers. By God's blessing, the government in America at that time was also friendly to the Islamic world, so a small power of Afghani Muslims defeated the largest power in the world, Russia.

"That's how these infidels were defeated in Afghanistan. This is when Pakistan became a real Islamic state. You can understand by this example, Brother Idrees, that 2 million kids were in madrassas at the time of Muhammad Zia-Ul-Haq, and that poor parents were very happy, because their kids were not only getting a free Islamic education, but also food, clothes, and a place to live.

"But then the incidents of September 11 happened, and by the plot of the Jews, all of the Anti-Islamic forces collected against Muslims. Then, one by one, they started to attack Muslim countries. First, they attacked Iraq, and then Afghanistan. Unfortunately, Pakistan was also governed by Musharraf's infidel government at that time, which was working on the Jews' agenda. So this is a tough time now on the Muslim *Ummah*. Saudi Arabia and our other brother Arab countries are united against this situation. Inshallah, one day, Islam will overcome again and the infidels will be defeated and insulted, as *Allah Tabarak'Tallah* promised the Muslims in the Quran."

After listening to all of this, the Mard-e-Momin, the symbolic Islamic man inside of Idrees was almost finished being cooked. Perhaps that was the reason why, a few days later, when Molvi Shamsul-Haq invited him to his villa for a special project, Idrees prepared himself for anything.

Chapter 20

Time: 10:30 am
Date: November 16, 2016
Location: Kabul, Afghanistan

Wahidi didn't feel comfortable talking about how he was injured. He diverted the bulk of Sania's nonstop questions by asking a question of his own.

"I am perfectly fine. I will tell you the details later. First you tell me about the matter you were intending to share with me. Is everything okay?"

In reply, Sania's fingers danced across the keyboard. *"Dr. Wahidi, first tell me; how would you define the difference between a good and a bad character?"*

"If you are hurt by another, physically or monetarily, it means that person's character isn't good. If you don't get hurt or if you actually benefit, it means the other person has a good character." Dr. Wahidi typed, answering her question as precisely as he could.

"Does society decide what our characters will be?"

"Yes, but it's not necessarily what would be correct for all societies. It is not always necessary that our character may be correct in our own society as well. If any act we do creates feelings of dissatisfaction in ourselves, we develop self-doubt through that act. The rest of our acts, those that relate to society, I consider artificial."

After thinking a moment, Wahidi continued. *"Look, Sania. We can't keep everyone in our society happy at the same time. I think if we keep ourselves up to basic ethical values, that would be quite enough."*

"Does a sexual act have any relation to being ethically right or wrong?"

Sania wrote his next answer cautiously. *"Human civilization evolved from an unknown to a known direction. The unknown era was the one that created the religious mindset. Naturally, religion utilized the sex drive to generate social-ethical values. As sex was not only a pleasurable drive but also instinctually connected with human regeneration, it played the same role in generating a kind of civilization both in animals and humans."*

Wahidi kept writing in the same flow and then stopped for a few seconds before resuming. When Sania realized that that Wahidi had not finished yet, she stopped her fingers and waited for his next message.

"Okay, answer my questions now. What do you think? Are religion and sex natural enemies, Sania?"

Sania thought for a second and then wrote, *"In my opinion, they are real enemies of each other. But please don't ask me why."*

During this, Daleep came to the living room holding a cup of tea in each hand and then sat by her on the sofa. He gave Sania a cup and began to read the chat with interest.

"Love is a natural drive involving very delicate feelings inside. We cannot analyze it mechanically. Sex is a very intense behaviour that can be analyzed mechanically. Love could be considered infinite in distance and shape, while sex has limited distance and shape. Look, Sania, religion cannot accommodate analysis in its nature, because an analytical mind will naturally not stay near religion. Religion utilized sex as a negative but love as a positive strength."

Sania thought about that for a moment and then wrote her next question. *"Does religion promote racism?"*

"Sania, a racist is basically a color-blind person. He can see only a few colors in the universe, which are selfishly connected to himself. These colors were politically created on the basis of skin, language, customs, traditions, geographic situation and culture, for the purpose of achieving economic benefit. There is no doubt that religion has a historical role in racism. In fact, if religion was against racism, it would not create terms and conditions to keep marriages in the same religion; it would not give priority to its own prophet; it would not promote its believers' own customs and prayers and compare them to other religions.

"Unfortunately, religion claims anti-racism but in fact promotes and spreads racism. We can blame negative politics for racism, but we need to think about it. How could a negative political process overcome a positive religious teaching so easily? There must be some defect in that teaching. That's why it was not only utilized easily but also entangled in politics. Then of course there would be many questions raised for the spiritual status of a religion, no?"

For some time there was a gap in their conversation. Perhaps Wahidi's last sentence provoked the opening of many intellectual doors for Sania and Daleep, and they were busy thinking about it. Before writing a response to "no?" Sania typed a direct question.

"Sir, once you told me that you were not able to marry the one you loved, and she was punished for it. She was falsely blamed for having a bad character, and both of you were attacked. That's how your parents and lover were killed. Was that the incident that made you rebel against religious school of thought?"

There was a short pause, and it looked to Sania that a few words were typed in the chatbox and then deleted, and then were retyped, word by word, and then deleted and again, words being typed one after the other.

Daleep and Sania were impatiently waiting for his reply, staring at the chatbox.

As Wahidi began to type, the computer screen gradually faded out and the Afghanistan of 1986 slowly appeared and spread itself across his vision.

It was the time when the replacement of Najeeb by Babrak Karmal had generated hope of some peace. But the Mujahideen refused to follow Babrak Karmal's command before signing the peace contract at Geneva. The Mujahideen drenched the Russian soldiers in blood during 1985 and 1986. They brutally targeted government offices, radio stations, air terminals, roads, bridges, cinema houses, electric power stations, industrial units and educational institutions with thousands of shells, rockets, bombs and grenades. As a consequence, the city was without electricity or water for many days. Grenades were exploding everywhere—on roads, streets, neighbourhoods and playgrounds, even in schools and colleges, killing citizens along with soldiers of the Soviet and Afghan army.

Compared to Kabul, Wahidi's province, Bamiyan, was more peaceful that year. There was no place other than Bamiyan for Wahidi to head to. The Kabul University was closed for months and he wasn't able to see Sofia for weeks.

On the other side, Sofia's life was also hell, because of her brother, Masood. Ever since he joined the Hezbe-Islami of *Gulbuddin Hekmatyar*, he had become very strict with Sofia. Sofia's father sometimes tried to resist him, but gradually he was also getting scared due to his son's aggressive behaviour.

Masood had advanced into Mujahideen activities. He was commanding one of their wings. Because of this, he was out of the home most of the time, but whenever he returned he controlled family members like they were also in his wing. Sofia's father was growing more helpless day by day, while Sofia's mother advised her not to go near her brother.

He still kept a strict eye on her, and not only verbally. Occasionally he physically abused her. Most of his anger at her came for her clothes and her leaving the house. He had become completely antagonistic towards her artwork. He knew that Sofia did her Bachelor's in Art, and painting was her passion. Now there was a stop sign for her Fine Arts. The suffocation was growing, as he was shouting at her and hurting her even more.

During this hard time, Wahidi's love was the only support in her life. With the help of Sherazi at his home, she used to meet Wahidi once every few weeks, but now she couldn't due to fear of Masood. Wahidi belonged to an Agha-khani Shia family, while Sofia grew up in an orthodox Sunni family. Sofia was born and grew up in Kabul, while Wahidi was a resident of Bamiyan, the province of Hazarajat. They differed, not only in their social and religious background but also in their Pakhtoon and Irani descent. This was not considered a big difference in Afghanistan before the Soviet war, but now the situation had changed. The difference had turned into a sin, which could be penalized with death. Wahidi was aware of this extremist wave, and he himself was finding it difficult, living in Afghanistan with this suffocation. Sometimes when he was alone, he thought that he would take Sofia with him and escape Afghanistan to a neighbouring country like Iran. He planned for his future life there, but…perhaps he shouldn't have done it in such a hurry.

If only that night Sofia hadn't left her house crying. Masood had beaten her, and she had left her house during the night and had come to see Sherazi's sister. Wahidi had met her there. If only he hadn't taken her with him to Bamiyan, the situation would have been different.

Wahidi and Sofia both knew that the road between Bamiyan to Kabul wasn't secure. That's why they took the road through Parwan instead of Wardak province. They changed buses three times, taking almost ten hours to get to Char Yakar and then Ghorbund before reaching Bamiyan.

That night, the whole village was drowned in darkness. Bamiyan's main bazar was in silence. The dim light of *kandil* lamps hanging out of houses tried to illuminate the road. The silence was occasionally broken by a sudden rush of dogs at each other, usually hiding under carts and behind the walls of shops. The yelps of a crying dog generated a depressing environment.

A storm of dust and the loud rattle of an engine arrived after midnight. Wahidi and Sofia had reached Bamiyan. The sound scared the dogs, and they went back to the shops and carts.

Wahidi's father had been running a big business selling dried fruit in the same main bazar for a long time. He was not only selling to the public but also supplying the smaller grocery stores nearby.

Bamiyan had a long, complex history of relationships with the other provinces of Afghanistan. Around a hundred years ago, during 1886, Hakim Abdul Rehman, a ruler of Afghanistan, had initiated a centralized movement of the state. He politically controlled several independent and semi-independent tribal groups, but for some reason, his behaviour was very aggressive and cruel with residents of the Hazara province. He took their land, made them slaves and then sold them or massacred them. In consequence, thousands of poor people escaped to Iran and migrated to the place that would become Pakistan in the future. The rest had become second- or third-class citizens and survived as labourers and servants. After a hundred years, during the Soviet Union's war, the extremist Mujahideen repeated the same history against the poor Shia residents of Hazara. They were always scared and experienced frequent attacks from this extremist group. This wasn't new for Wahidi—that's why he planned to stay one or two days with his parents, and after introducing Sofia to them, he had planned to cross the border into Iran.

That night, when Wahidi reached his muddy home, a small suitcase in one hand and Sofia's hand in the other, his parents had been scared instead of happy to see him. Especially his father, who was well aware of the Mujahideen's influence over Hazara. He thought that his son had made two big mistakes. First of all, he had brought a girl from a Sunni sect from Kabul without a *nikha*. Second, they had come to Bamiyan, which was more dangerous than Kabul itself.

Wahidi's father told him that Bamiyan wasn't like it used to be. There was no peace at all. The situation could suddenly switch into chaos in Maidan Wardak, Ghor and Rosegan, and then spread to Bamiyan because of the clashes amongst the Mujahideen, Tanzeem Nasal No Hazara, Khomeni Islamic Group and the ruling party. The terrorist groups of Gulbadin Hikmat Yar were present all over and fighting in the front lines during every clash.

Wahidi's father had been right. The Mujahideen intelligence had been quicker than the romantic dreams of Wahidi and Sofia. Immediately after they left Kabul, Sherazi was kidnapped. The next night, even before Wahidi woke up, Masood and numerous other Mujahideen fighters reached Bamiyan. There was a cry of "Allah-Hu-Akbar" and a burst from a Kalashnikov struck the chests of Wahidi, Sofia, and his parents. The firing was so heavy that his parents and Sofia died immediately. Wadidi was wounded, but he survived because they moved on, assuming he was dead.

Wahidi hadn't thought that all of this would happen so quickly. Otherwise, he would never have brought Sofia to Bamiyan, and his parents and Sofia would not have suffered due to his mistake.

Wahidi's wounds hadn't even healed when he heard that Masood was also killed in a clash between the Soviet Union army and the Mujahideen, but by then it was far too late.

Wahidi wiped the computer screen with his hand, but it was still blurry. Then he wiped his eyes and began to type.

"No, Sania, it isn't like that. I'm that lucky one who has grown up under the shade of the great statues of Buddha. When I was young, I used to sit by the feet of Solsol and Shahmama, and I asked Buddha, "If there is no concept of god in Buddhism, and your teachings are always against

idol worship...then why have your disciples made your statues for worship? Is it because the human is naturally inclined to worship?

"Sania, you belong to the new generation of the 21st century, and you want to be a psychologist as your occupation. In that case, you need to find the reality of inner truth through scientific consciousness instead of through a religious mindset of the time of before Christ. It could be possible that the spiritual drive of human intellect may entrap you in its complex net without the help of organized religion. But I have a belief that the modern analytical difference between the soul and the mind will take you ahead to a conscious destiny, which has never been reached by your ancestors before Christ. Trust me, it is possible. Consciousness depends only on the light of knowledge, and you're lucky to be born in the enlightened, scientific world of the 21st century, not during the dark tomb of the ignorant past. Okay, Sania. Let me leave now. I'm feeling tired because of the pain of my past. I'll talk to you later."

After saying this, Wahidi turned off the computer.

Chapter 21

Time: 11 pm
Date: November 21, 2017
Location: Shah Faisal Colony, Karachi, Pakistan

Breaking news flashed on the TV when Bakhtawar turned it on. The bulletin was about an extremist attack on a Mosque. According to the newscaster, numerous terrorists entered the Mosque from the back door and began shooting at those praying, who were bowing during the *Rukū'*. The attack was so sudden and severe that eleven worshippers were immediately killed while 36 were horribly injured. The death toll was increasing every second. The screen showed photos of the injured and dead. The floors and the walls of the mosque were running red with human blood. The flesh of the human body and chunks of brain had scattered all over. Prayer mats and the pages of Quran, soaked with blood, were spread everywhere. Friends and relatives of the victims were crying loudly as they placed the injured into ambulances and private cars that would rush them to the hospital.

When Bakhtawar anxiously raised the TV volume, the voice of the newscaster, the screams of crying people and the sounds of ambulances all together filled the room with noise. In the corner of the room, Usman stared at the TV, terrified. He felt that the flowing blood of the mosque was oozing out of the screen and into the room. Drop by drop, the blood became waves, the torn flesh floating on it, and the dead bodies were flowing onto the carpet. Like a storm in a river, it stuck to Bakhtawar, and without making her wet started flowing towards Usman.

Usman began crying and shouting in panic. The blood was spreading all over the room and gradually filling it up. He felt himself drowning in the blood, and he couldn't breathe. He screamed hysterically.

Bakhtawar turned around and saw his fright.

She then looked back to the TV screen, full of blood and dead bodies, and realized that the news was causing his hysterical attack. Immediately she stood up and turned off the TV. She then looked back to the frightened boy and tried to grab him. When Usman saw Bakhtawar coming for him, he was scared even more and cringed back. He thought that Bakhtawar was one of the dead victims. When he found a wall behind him, he stared at her with frightened eyes, taking deep breaths.

She tried to grab him, but he tried to escape from her hands. Then he suddenly turned around and grabbed her instead, shouting like a drowning person clutching a lifeguard.

Bakhtawar picked up Usman and ran out to the veranda. Then she thought of something. Leaving him on the veranda, she returned to the room and found the medication his doctor advised her to give him immediately during a hysterical attack. She threw a tablet into his mouth and then poured water in to wash it down. But the way Usman was gasping and writhing, it was almost impossible to get him to swallow any medication.

Bakhtawar then tried to call Idrees, but found his phone was turned off. She didn't waste any time. She put on a *burqa* and ran to the home of her neighbour, Ghazi Salahuddin, so she could use his car to take Usman to the clinic.

But the doctor in the clinic couldn't manage Usman's complex hysteric attacks, so she took him to the neighbouring hospital where she could find someone to help him. She tried to phone Idrees again and left him a message about taking Usman to the emergency ward of the hospital.

By the time he got the message, Idrees had returned home and was looking around the empty house. He went outside, locked the door, turned around and began to run to the hospital. After a few steps on the street, he had a thought and returned home. There, he closed all the doors and windows. He then took out the shotgun concealed under the robe of his shalwar and locked it in the cupboard.

He locked the front door of his house again, ran quickly into the street and disappeared in the dark.

Chapter 22

Time: 4:00 pm
Date: November 21, 2016
Location: Mississauga, Canada

"Okay, then, see you tomorrow at the university."

Saying this, Daleep hung up the phone and turned to Sania.

He laughed at himself. "These days, boys are talking more than girls." He shrugged, coming back to the living room to sit on the sofa where Sania was reviewing a few of his written assignments. Sania looked towards Daleep and smiled, then focused back on the file. As she flipped a page, Daleep's cell phone started ringing.

She picked up the phone and read the caller ID. "Abbaji's calling!" Sometimes Daleep's mother called on the same line, but since Daleep had been trying to call his father lately, she was right about Abbaji calling back.

Daleep and his father conversed in their native language, but by now Sania was able to understand Punjabi, though she wasn't able to speak it.

After Daleep turned off the phone, Sania looked up from the papers. "So what was Abbaji saying?"

Daleep walked to the kitchen and put his tea into the microwave, pressing the temperature button for 40 seconds. He kept staring blankly at the tea in the microwave. He then walked back to the living room and sat beside Sania.

"Sania, Abbaji said what I thought he would say. He's a very broad-minded man. After listening to everything, he said, 'Look son, Nanak Dev ji said that we should be human beings before becoming Hindu, Muslim, Sikh, or Christians. And the one who finds love… has found God. If you feel that your love is true, then keep her in your heart and respect her. Son, you are lucky. About the other problems, don't worry. All of these issues fade away in the dust of time. Your mother is a traditional type of person. Perhaps it will be hard for her to digest. But don't worry, son. As time passes, people make many compromises in life.

"'Even so, my advice is not to be too rushed in any decision. Sometimes, something that we see from afar is different when we see it nearby. It's also a blessing that both of you are with each other. It's good that you can understand each other, and realize that whatever you think about each other at a distance is the same when you are close to each other, so that you know it wasn't just an emotional burst.

"'Son, when we live with someone, we find out more about them. Just respect each other…what else can I advise? You're already an educated and mature person. God bless you. And yes, I will try to explain it to your mother gradually, but it may take some time.'"

Sania looked at him with a smile. "That's great. I'm surprised, Daleep. You're a lucky man. I wish my father was like yours so that half our problem would be solved."

Daleep cut her short. "Your parents are visiting here tomorrow. When will they be here?"

"Yeah, tomorrow morning you meet them for the first time. I'm scared there's going to be a big mess. Well, let's see."

Sania took an anxious breath. She stared silently at the papers in front of her.

* * *

110

The next day, Sania's parents sat on the same sofa where she and Daleep had been sitting the night before, worrying about the consequences of this meeting.

Sania's mother looked into her eyes and said, 'Sania, what have you decided? How long will this episode continue?'

"I think we should talk to Daleep sahib instead of Sania," Sania's father gritted his teeth and muttered without listening to Sania's reply, his eyes showing anger and frustration.

Daleep looked at Sania's father, then lowered his head again. For a second he felt that he had committed an unknown sin and called it love. *Maybe I should ask Professor Wahidi about ethically analyzing love… a background of meaningless words like "sin" and "reward", and meaningful words like "love." Weren't these sins and rewards the initial words beginning the exploitation of human intellect?*

Daleep was beginning to realize that his love of Sania was opening the door of a mysterious world he had never been to before. Whatever he had heard about Wahidi from Sania had deeply attached him to this unknown intellectual. He wanted to sit down with Professor Wahidi to discuss topics he had never found in a medical book. It would be impossible to understand human science without this knowledge.

Then he was back from the dispersed, romantic, colorful world of Wahidi, into the bitter world of Sania's parents, where the decision about his genuine emotions would be judged on the basis of religion and nationalism.

"Daleep, sahib, Sania's mother has told me that you're a medical student?"

"Yes." Daleep replied, confidently but also politely. "I've almost completed medical school this year."

Sania's father picked a question out of his collection of thoughts.

"Are you here on a student visa?"

Daleep caught the trend of his thoughts and said, smiling, "Yes, I'm on a student visa."

"So, what're you going to do? Your education is finished here."

"Well, my post-graduate work will start next year at McMaster University. It's a four-year training course, and after that I want to complete a fellowship in Cardiology. I'm still in Canada for another seven years."

This was new information for Sania's parents because they had a very limited knowledge of medical school. They didn't understand that in order to become a cardiologist, one should have eleven years of education after a four-year BSc. They had come to Canada fourteen years ago after Sania's father took a total of four years of BSc and MSc in computer sciences from Pakistan and then completed one more year of MSc at the Carleton University of Ottawa. He was always proud of his academic achievement.

After hearing Daleep's career plan, Sania's parents looked at him in a new light. He was a tall, good-looking young man of 26, with a lot of intelligence in his eyes. His outfit was typical of Sikhs, with a turban on his head and a light beard. But his face was full of innocence.

If Daleep's beard and turban were to be removed, he would look like a very handsome man, Sania's father thought. He then looked towards Sania's mom, trying to tell her something through his eyes. He cleared his throat.

"Look, Daleep. We know that you and Sania are serious about each other. And we also would like to put personal emotions aside before we decide. Fact is, we don't want this situation to continue, because we are being defamed. Gossip is spreading around our community…that our daughter is living with someone. In fact, we can't tolerate it at all. Besides religion, we also have family traditions, and living in the West doesn't mean that we will adopt their bad values alongside the good ones.

"I'll be straightforward; first of all, we'd like to take Sania back home to live with us. After thinking for a bit, we've decided that if you become an Ahmadi Muslim and read the Kalma with an honest heart, we may consider accepting you into our family, considering our daughter's emotions. Although," he took a deep breath, "we still have a lot of issues there. For example, there's a big difference of culture between us. We came to Karachi after migrating from Delhi, while you are from Eastern Punjab. There's a difference in our culture, tradition, and values. We would also want you to live in Canada after marriage with Sania and forget going back to Punjab and living there. If you accept these conditions, then we may consider you. We are talking about these considerations because we still need to discuss with our family and community."

Before Daleep could say anything, Sania said, "But Daddy, this isn't fair."

But Daleep waved his hand, asking her to stop. "Could you give us some time to think about this?"

Sania's mother looked at Sania's father with surprise. The things he was saying hadn't been mentioned at home. Accepting Daleep into the family as Sania's husband was completely new for her.

But Sania's father said in a very soft tone. "Yes, yes, why not? But Sania, please. Let's go home."

Sania's mother agreed and said, "Without you, our home has become empty. Come along with us."

But Sania replied, "No, mom. Not at this time. I will not come home until everything is decided."

Both of them regarded Sania, and after a few seconds her father shrugged and stood up.

"Okay, as you like." He looked at his wife. "I think we should leave now." He regarded both of them, and said, "Whatever you decide, let us know."

Saying this, he indicated that his wife should move.

Sania looked towards Daleep, who seemed to be peacefully staring at the floor, but he was trapped in the complex net of his deep thoughts.

Chapter 23

Time: 11:00 pm
Date: November 21, 2016
Location: Kabul, Afghanistan

Wahidi had spent over a week at the residence of Nazir Azizi. He still hadn't settled down from the attack at his house. He was becoming anxious to move back home as soon as possible, and one day he took out his bag and started to pack.

"Are you going back home already? Don't you think it's too soon?" Nazir Azizi asked, surprised.

"No, Nazir. I have a lot of incomplete assignments to finish back home. I'd love to stay with you but the way things are piling up, it would be tough to compensate for it."

Nazir agreed and offered to drop him at home.

Once he reached home, he felt frustrated because of the loneliness, but soon became busy in his schedule as usual. He had decided he would start on his new book, *The Evolution of Afghanistan: From Buddha to Osama*. He had written a lot, but still felt that it wasn't enough. He needed much more historical, political, social, and religious references on this topic, which required time spent in the Central Kabul library and a visit to other areas in Afghanistan to gather documentary facts.

Because of the events of the previous few weeks, he hadn't found time to work on this important subject. Last week at Nazir Azizi's home he had been distracted because of the thoughts wandering about his mind and painful memories from the past stabbing at his soul. After talking to

Sania, his heart had been loaded. Now he believed that his past had become his present, otherwise he wouldn't be sad for so many days after a brief chat with Sania on Facebook. But the pain of his past had become the strength of his present and his future or he would have killed himself already.

Why is Sania asking this kind of question? he thought when he reached home. *Perhaps there is a conflict in her life that she needs a way to get out of, and she is trapped somewhere between two different passages of her heart.* He remembered Sofia asking him the same question 25 years ago when she had come crying to Sherazi's home. Sofia's family had followed the custom of tribal marriages. He was not only a complete Afghani pakhtun but also his background was Iranian Shia Muslim. Were these really important questions in the matter of their love? That night, Sofia had looked into his eyes and asked the same question.

"And I don't know what she saw in my eyes…what made her place her finger on my lips and gently say, 'Don't speak, Wahidi…please. My question itself is becoming a crime against my love.'"

Were Sofia and Sania two passengers going down the same road? Racial and religious hatred had inflicted so much pain on delicate human emotions, exploiting the proper evolutionary process of culture…contaminating human emotions for its own selfish survival.

And now, in the form of Sania, it placed his memories of Sofia at the front of a similar frightening situation after two decades…with the same result to be expected.

Why isn't there a specific name for an ethos created by this cross of race and religion?

Why isn't there a specific name for human feelings being created by this corrupted mindset?

Why isn't there a specific name for human emotions being created by all these contaminated feelings?

Why isn't there a specific name for the consequences created by all these emotions and feelings?

Or maybe…

…there is a name.

Wahidi smiled and murmured to himself, "Our world's civilization."

He looked around, then breathed a sigh of relief. Good thing nobody else was nearby. People would laugh at him, seeing him talking to himself. His train of thought was running nonstop when his cell phone rang.

Nazir Azizi was on the other end.

"Listen, I have bad news and good news for you. What do you want to hear first?"

"Tell me the bad news first, so I can hear the good news with all of my heart."

"The bad news is that the Taliban have planned to start killing off the liberal, secular intellectual writers and journalists of Afghanistan, and unfortunately, your name is on their list. It means that whatever happened to you over the past few days was part of that plan. It wasn't because of your articles, but because of the Taliban's opinion of you: secular, an atheist and one of their enemies." Nazir said it all in one breath.

"I was also beginning to feel like that. The way they found my address and attacked me…the way they threatened me over the phone…it was really serious in nature. Now, tell me the good news?" Wahidi asked in a calm tone.

Nazir Azizi's voice rose in excitement. "The good news is that the University of California has chosen you for a political-social lecture on behalf of Kabul University. The topic is Afghanistan and the Global World, and lectures will be arranged in California as well as Washington, DC. There's a program in the UK, too, arranged in collaboration with the University of Manchester. Our vice-chancellor has all the information. I hope he will talk to you about your availability soon because the program starts within the next week. I'm pretty sure the university is arranging your visa and airline ticket in the next few days, but it all depends on your interest."

"What do you think about it?" Wahidi asked slowly.

"You should go. First of all, it's a good opportunity to talk openly about the problems of Afghanistan at an international level, and place your opinion in front of the world. Secondly, it's a good reason to get out of the painful environment around here. Let me tell you this; don't even think about coming back as long as your life is threatened here. In fact, you should stay there until the atmosphere in Afghanistan gets better,"

Wahidi took a deep sigh, "Okay, I'll think about it. I'll see you tomorrow at the University." Turning off the phone, Wahidi looked over the files scattered across his desk and pulled one out. He skimmed through the pages and started crossing out some sentences and marking stars next to others:

"During the evolutionary process, human beings have established national states for their own survival in the form of a group, allowing them to grow up. But this self and general growth and success later turn into the feeling of self-importance and a superiority complex. Our feelings of association for a specific nation are usually developed after a certain age because we develop long memories and a level of convenience or habit of living in the same culture for years. Love itself is a natural emotion, but its strings have become tangled with many unnatural elements. The ethos of nationalism is absolutely artificial. In the name of the nation or the country, to kill another human being and then label these murders in the name of nationalism is the bankruptcy of ethics. Patriotism is an extreme version of nationalism. The wildest emotions of hatred, murder and bloodshed hide deep inside its soul.

Globalization has no negative impact on nationalism, but creates a new kind of challenge for it. We can see that the extreme form of this challenge in the immigrant families of North America and England, whose children have more connections with religion than with their place of birth. Thus they raise weapons against their own country because of their connection with the *Daesh* and ISI. Nationalism actually dies when it crosses religion."

Wahidi circled words while reading these sentences. There was room for improvement in the article.

At last, he decided to close the file, turn on his computer and check his e-mail.

Chapter 24

Time: 2:00 am
Date: November 22, 2016
Location: Shah Faisal Colony, Karachi, Pakistan

After checking Usman, the doctor took Bakhtawar aside. "He has had a mental shock. I have given him medicine. He'll be all right soon."

Bakhtawar, shaken, looked up at him with a child-like expression. "Doctor, can I ask you something?"

The doctor replied politely, "Yes, yes, please."

"Doctor, my son was completely normal before he suddenly developed these attacks. Before he was just throwing up, now he sees things…sometimes he hears voices too. Today his body started jerking around so violently that he became short of breath. He felt as if he was suffocating. Doctor sahib, do you think an evil spirit has entered him? That happened to the child of a distant relative. They took him to an *amil,* a spiritualist, an expert at removing ghosts from the body. That's how he was relieved."

After hearing this, the doctor made a face and said with a slight smile,

"Listen, madam. Your child is having a panic attack. Patients develop symptoms of psychosis during an extreme hysteric attack. The things your child was seeing and hearing were just hallucinations. These are very common in this kind of situation. None of it is in the real world that you can see or hear. The patient feels like there's a whole different world around him. That's what makes him see and hear things that don't exist.

All of this is because of the imbalance of neurotransmitters because of the extreme effects of the shock. It could be managed with medication, but there is no guarantee that these signs won't develop again. The most important thing is to keep him away from the type of thing that may develop the hysteric attack. By the way, can I ask you something?"

"Oh, yes, Doctor sahib." Bakhtawar said enthusiastically.

"Do you have any family history of this kind of hysteric attack? Especially in close family members?"

Bakhtawar fell deep into thought. She knew there was nobody in her family, but she didn't know about Idrees' family.

"Well…as far as I remember there's nobody. But I'll ask my husband. If there is, does it make any difference?" She said reluctantly. "Is it possible that he'll come back to normal and never become like this again ?"

"Look, if there are psychological diseases present in a family, then members of that family have some psychotic issues that become more exposed in vulnerable situations. But if the patient takes medications on time, there is a good chance for improvement. I would suggest you bring him to my office in a week."

As the doctor finished speaking, Idrees rushed into the clinic and anxiously asked his wife, "Bakhtawar, is everything all right? How's Usman?" He put his hand on the forehead of his son, who was in a deep sleep because of the medication. The doctor turned towards Idrees and then left the room immediately. Perhaps he was in a hurry to see other patients, and he didn't want to tell Idrees the same things he just said to Bakhtawar.

"Is everything all right? What happened? What's the doctor saying?"

Bakhtawar looked at Idrees. "Oh, thank God. Everything is okay. Suddenly he developed the same kind of fit he had before. This time he lost breath, and I was scared. I felt like he was suffocating. That's why I ran to our neighbour, Salahuddin *bhai*. Thank God he was at home and he brought me to this hospital immediately. The emergency doctor downstairs said to me that this is a psychological case of fits. It could only be treated by a psychiatrist. Luckily, there was a psychiatrist here now. The physician in the emergency room was saying that there are many of the same kind of cases coming to the hospital nowadays. Especially young children. A lot of psychological issues. That's why now we have a psychiatrist available."

Idrees was frustrated by her long talk, "Okay, okay. Leave the story and tell me; what was the doctor saying about our Usman? Is he going to be okay or not?"

Bakhtawar shrugged. "Well, now he's been given medication. Since then, there've been no more fits."

"Doctor sahib didn't admit him into the hospital?"

"Oh, no. They said to take him home and bring him back in a week for another check-up."

Hearing this, Idrees lifted Usman from the hospital bed.

Outside the hospital, Salahuddin sahib was waiting in his car. When he saw Idrees and Bakhtawar coming, he got out and opened the back door and helped Idrees put Usman into the car.

'Idrees *Bhai*, how is Usman now?' Salahuddin asked.

Idrees replied, "Well, Salahuddin. I couldn't understand this doctor talk. Sometimes they say they'll be better for good. Other times they say come back later. I think it's all because they want your money. See, the emergency doctor takes 1000 rupees. The psychiatrist took 3000 rupees to see him, 2000 rupees for the medicine, and then said to come back later. They said there's no guarantee of full recovery."

Salahuddin drove the car, wondering about how Idrees could afford all of these heavy expenses. Idrees kept talking about how expensive the doctors were. Bakhtawar's fingers ran through Usman's hair. Salahuddin cringed when he heard Idrees' voice again.

"I don't think these doctors will offer anything other than a tranquilizer and sleep medication for my son."

"Why so, Idrees?" Salahuddin asked, absent-mindedly. He was still thinking about where he was getting the funds to pay the big bills.

"All they're doing is drawing more money into their wallets," Idrees replied, without realizing that Salahuddin was also thinking about money.

Reaching home, Idrees was laying Usman on the bed when his cell phone rang. It was Molvi Salimullah calling to say that Molvi Sirajul-Haq wanted to see Idrees right away at his home.

After hanging up the phone, he said to Bakhtawar:

"Molvi Sirajul-Haq has just asked me to visit him." He looked at Usman. "What you were saying just now…about how he was seeing faces and hearing sounds…I have the same opinion about both. All of these issues are from *jina*…ghosts. I'll consult Molvi Sirajul-Haq. He, himself is a learned religious scholar. Perhaps he'll suggest some verses to relieve the problem. Even so, anything can be treated with the Quran. Otherwise, what are these ghosts gonna do to my kid?"

Idrees put his hand with confidence onto Usman's head and spoke again to Bakhtawar:

"Okay, I'm leaving. I might be late coming home."

"Okay…but at least eat something before you go," Bakhtawar said.

"No-no, I'll grab something with Molvi Salim on the way to Molvi Sirajul-Haq's home. For now, you just look after Usman."

As Bakhtawar was closing the door behind him, Idrees suddenly turned around and whispered into her ear, "Oh, Allah. In all of this mess I left out the good news. Molvi Salimullah has said that he'll buy us some land for a cheap price in the area of Orangi town. There's a mosque *dinyat* there. It's like the same mosque we have here in our neighbourhood…actually a branch of that mosque. There's some empty place near the mosque of a few acres. They would like to keep their own people around the mosque…that's why they're asking me to move there, so that we could catch anyone causing an evil act. I'll have to run the administration there. I immediately agreed…it's almost a free-of-cost plot. We'll construct a great home on it later."

Bakhtawar was very happy hearing this. "Such good news. I'm sure this is all a blessing from Allah." She put her hands together as if she was praying: "What someone said was true: There can be a delay, but never a darkness."

After Idrees left, Bakhtawar closed the door and, lost in her thoughts, came back into the room. She was pleased to think about how her life had changed in the last few weeks. She could never have thought that this was the same Idrees who used to just wander around, interfering in other people's business and causing trouble. Now, everything had changed radically…in such a good way. Only a few months ago, Idrees couldn't even earn a penny doing manual jobs around the community…painting peoples' walls, fixing faucets and electrical switches to make enough to survive. It was quite expensive, paying hydro bills and buying groceries. There was always arguing, fighting about small chores, crying, shouting and beating at home. So much stress.

But now, within three weeks! We even have air conditioning. A fridge. And now Idrees is planning to buy a car. He talks about a plot of land as well. If Allah helps, I'm sure we'll have a very good house in a good place, and we'll be free of this rental land. Maybe that area will be better than this place.

A million thanks to God. I Just want Usman to get better soon. Oh, Allah...the way you've sent blessings into Idrees' heart, and have brought him to the right pathway... I can see Idrees now praying five times a day. That must be the source of all the blessings in our home. I was right that there's no darkness in His home.

As she entered the room, she turned on the TV without a second thought. Then, noticing Usman sleeping on the bed, she remembered everything quickly and turned off the TV.

Chapter 25

Time: 7:00 pm
Date: November 27, 2016
Location: Mississauga, Canada

Daleep's meeting with Sania's parents opened a new window in his mind. He had never thought what he would do in such a situation. He asked himself several times. *Could I become a Muslim for Sania?*

Accepting that he loved Sania, what would happen if she left his life? Possibly he would marry a girl selected by Beji. The girl would be Sikh and Punjabi like him, and all of his family members would be very happy, since she would be just like them, top to bottom. It was also possible that he would get married to a Punjabi Sikh doctor, earn a lot of money, and both of them would be very rich. It was also possible that he'd be wed into an upper-class family. Maybe the daughter of a bureaucrat in the Punjabi government, or even a minister. That would bring status and money into his life.

Another fact was that he would soon be a cardiologist, and a qualification like that was in high demand in India. Once Beji told him that the girl's family pays a dowry of 500,000 rupees for a boy who's an Indian doctor, while an American-Canadian doctor gets much more. She was so happy when she found out he was accepted into a medical school in Canada, her mouth was full of words.

"Daleep has changed our life! By the blessings of Guru ji, *Bhagwan* has given us such an excellent boy!"

It was also possible that he would forget Sania after a few days. Who could remember someone while he was busy with work and family? Everyone's lives are almost the same, day or night. When he thought about nighttime, something pinched deep in his throat. His heart trembled.

He felt that a thorn had grown out from a corner of his heart and was stuck in his throat. *It will only be me in the night. During the day I'll be busy in the hospital with the patients and the staff with whom I'm involved for my professional duties. They'll only meet me like they meet other doctors. But in the evening I'll be with my kids, and it might be okay that these kids aren't from Sania, because they're my kids. So I could love them, and take care of them, and raise them and fulfill my responsibilities.*

When I go to the bank, I'll be very happy with the number of dollars in my account. I could invest that money after putting it into my children's accounts for the sake of their careers. And when I meet someone at a party with friends, I'll talk to them a lot. I may forget everything... other than the pain. And what about the night? I'll be alone... only I will be there. Only me. With myself. Alone... I couldn't be with Sania, to whom I say everything, openly, without second thought.

Possibly I will marry the most beautiful, educated rich girl. But then... would she be like Sania? Like my own Sania? All day I'll be fixing my patients' hearts through mechanical means, but during the night? Will I try to fix my heart? Would I be able to cement it together? What if I'm unable to?

I have to decide... what am I going to do with my life?

Where am I going to live, with my heart or with its pulse?

Do I want to live with the pain, or the ache?

Do I want to live with myself or with others?

I can lie to anyone in the entire world... but can I lie to myself?

Maybe I can live without Sania by staying up every night of my life. And maybe I can live my life fulfilling dreams of which not one would be my own.

Even so, I was never one to dream in the night. All of my dreams were seen in the morning, going towards the coming days.

No, no. This is very difficult. I cannot marry anyone other than Sania. So, would I convert to Muslim because of Sania? Then... what's going to happen? Will I leave my family's religion for my love?

Dad once told me that Guru Nanak said, "Before being Hindu, Muslim, Sikh, or Christian, we should be human. The one who finds love finds his God." I think I should be a human being before being a Sikh or a Muslim. If I stay Sikh, and live my life with someone without loving her, I continue to lie to myself. Day and night.

If I spend my days lying to someone that I love her, then would my Bhagwan, *my God, be happy with me? My* Bhagwan *knows that I love Sania with my true heart.*

It must be that God, or Bhagwan, *if they're really around, then they must be in the form of love and humanity. Otherwise, the leftover traditions, cultures, and values are all created by human beings. These are all artificial, period. To be a Sikh or Muslim is not important. The importance is... how human are we? These religions... Sikh, Muslim, Hindu, and Jew... all of these just divide human beings... causing hatred. This is why it's not a true God. Actually... I think there's no God at all. If there's no love in them, they're just words. No humanity. The people following these divisions unfortunately don't understand religion, God, or* Bhagwan *at all. They're innocent people who are victimized by the artificial thinking of religion. This is all political and social division... and nothing. My only God is the feeling of my love and my service to humanity. My services to humanity and my services to human beings are my services to God. All of my days will go with the pain of patients and all of my nights will be with someone who is a true person in my life. Do I need anything extra in my life?*

Daleep was trapped in the network of these thoughts for days.

Sania had noticed that ever since her parents had met Daleep, he had been quiet and withdrawn. In fact, she welcomed this, so he could think more seriously and reach a final conclusion.

One evening, when Daleep was lost in his thoughts, standing alone in the corner of their balcony, Sania silently came behind him and took his hand.

"Daleep, I'm an Ahmadi Muslim and you're a Punjabi Sikh. Is this division stronger than the sum of our love?"

Daleep put his finger on her lips and spoke softly,

"No…and that's why I'm ready to change into a Muslim."

When Sania heard this, her eyes filled with tears. She set his finger aside and kissed him on the lips. They stood embracing for a long time, there on the balcony, kissing each other and crying together.

After a few seconds, Sania softly said to Daleep: "Let's go inside. I've made tea for you."

Chapter 26

Time: 7:30 a.m.
Date: November 27, 2016
Location: Kabul, Afghanistan

At the Kabul Airport, the vice chancellor of Kabul University and some of the professors had arrived to say goodbye to Wahidi. Wahidi spoke aside to Nazir. "If you were with me it would have been better."

Nazir Azizi replied with a smile, "Next time, *inshallah.* So what's the airline schedule? What airline are you using? When are you going to be there?"

"Oh, it's Turkish Airlines. We'll get to Istanbul in 6 hours."

Wahidi put his right hand on Nazir's shoulder. "We stay there for three or four hours, and the next leg of the journey is to JFK, in New York. I have to stay in New York for a night in a hotel. The next day there's a flight to Washington, where someone will pick me up and take me to the hotel where I'll stay for four days. Then I'll see what happens next."

"Have a safe trip," Nazir hugged him. "Hey, man, keep in touch. I'll update you about what happens here."

"Definitely." Wahidi waved to all of his friends and walked towards the boarding gate.

Soon, Wahidi was in the air, reading through some of his previous articles.

Then he remembered the lecture, "Afghanistan and the Global World," that he planned to give at the University of California. Thinking about this, he smiled. *Inside the bazaar of this new, global market economy, where do we place the spoiled boxes—the underdeveloped countries—to sell?*

Why not put the words in my head on paper? I'll add them into my article once I reach Washington.

Wahidi's pen was like a paddle propelling him through a sea of paper:

"For the last four decades, Afghanistan has been intensively involved with both capitalist and non-capitalist powers. As a consequence, Afghanistan has been destroyed economically and politically. In order to defeat anti-capitalist power, capitalist forces utilized a non-religious state, like China, and religious states like Saudi Arabia to implant an artificial ji*hadi* culture—with the help of a client state, Pakistan—into Afghanistan.

And right when the crops were ready, in order to destroy them, the capitalists replanted an anti-*Jihadi* culture. If the Afghan nation were able to use their political intellectuals to interpret modern social, economic, and religious concepts instead of keeping the heart-grown, decayed idea of religion and nationalism, then perhaps they could have saved themselves from joining either the capitalist or anti-capitalist forces, and Afghanistan would never have turned into the failed state it is today.

In addition to the traditional concept of religion and nationalism, Afghanistan is facing the challenges of a cultural, political, and economic situation, as well as keeping itself alive in the global world.

Besides nationalism, religions have also been political merchandise in the economic world. Weren't millions of Jews burned by Christians in Europe? And then, didn't the Christians themselves kill each other for centuries? And today, in the Middle East, aren't Muslims decapitating and burning each other alive?

To get economic benefits, religious ethical values were always used to rationalize wars, because these ethical values were not only very fragile but also could be easily manipulated. In the world of technology and the era of globalization, religion should be taught in the form of human values, respect, and freedom of expression, instead of a package of sins and deeds. Why shouldn't we interpret religion by the freedom of meanings instead of the cement of words so that we develop one global religion called humanity? Social and political interpretations have removed the spirituality from religion and tossed humanity into a world of hatred instead of love.

We should be like Leo Tolstoy, Martin Luther King and Gandhi, and remove the radicalism and violence from religion and develop a new identity."

After writing this, Wahidi took a deep breath and smiled. *It's so easy to write and speak all of this, but how difficult it is to imagine a world without any religion or nationalism! Hitler turned religion and nationalism into one and soaked his hands in the blood of millions of innocent human beings. Arabs turned radical Wahhabism and racist nationalism into one and soaked their hands in the blood of underdeveloped Islamic countries.*

Within a few seconds, his mind slipped back to something he read twenty years ago. In Jeff McMahan's book, *The Morality of Nationalism*, he recalled an interesting article by Robert Godden: "Why Is Nationalism Sometimes So Nasty?" Wahidi frequently referenced this article to his students. To introduce the article, he often said, "For years we have consciously used the glue of nationalism to stick the pages of race, place, religion and history into the envelope of our so-called community."

Wahidi didn't realize that his eyes had closed as he fell into the distracted thoughts of religion and nationalism.

When he opened his eyes, the plane was half an hour away from Istanbul. The air hostess had found him sleeping and decided not to wake him up, serving tea to the passenger beside him.

Wahidi woke up with a yawn, gathering his scattered papers and putting them back in his leather bag.

He pressed a button and called a hostess to order a cup of tea as well.

Soon the plane landed in Istanbul. Wahidi was standing at one of the bookshops in the airport skimming through numerous books when his eyes fell upon *My Stroke of Insight*, a book by an American writer, jill Bolte Taylor.

The description on the back of the book was interesting. The writer had a background in neurosciences. She had experienced a brain stroke and analyzed the spiritual experiences that happened throughout.

Wahidi thought, *Let's see what the scientific mind says about spirituality.*

Purchasing the book, Wahidi placed it into his bag so that the trip from Istanbul to New York could be a memorable one.

When he reached the waiting lounge, Wahidi turned on his laptop, opened Facebook and sent Sania a message:

"Thought I should let you know. I am just leaving for a conference in Washington."

Chapter 27

Time: 3:00 am
Date: November 22, 2016
Location: Defence Society, Karachi, Pakistan

There was quite the noise at Molvi Sirajul-Haq's home. In addition to Molvi Salimullah, ten people had gathered. There was a certain shine in everyone's faces, and they were all congratulating each other about the successful mission.

As soon as Molvi Sirajul-Haq found Idrees coming into the living room, he exclaimed, *"Masha'Allah,* our seventh *jihadi* has arrived! Step forward and give him a good hug."

Idrees embraced everyone in the room and then sat down on the carpet alongside Molvi Salimullah.

"My brothers; at this moment, fifteen Shia *kafir* have been sent to hell. Eight of them are seriously wounded, and twenty-five or twenty-six are injured. All of our Muslim brothers have come back as victors, *ghazi,* of Islam! This is what we call planning and teaching our enemies a lesson! By God, we are glad that Islam has such soldiers willing to risk their lives. And thank God that brother Idrees is alongside us in this holy work. This is the second great deed by our brother, *ghazi* Muhammad Idrees! Allah ease his paths for him in the future and keep him on the righteous way, as he is now, in the future battle between evil and good. All right, brothers, let us have dinner.

"Just as I advised you before, you all should move to different centres in Punjab. There, all of your living, eating, and resting has been accounted for. This is because the enemies of Islam will try to get you arrested and take 'legal' action to show the world. But we don't want anything interfering with the success of our mission, or any damage to our soldiers from these *kafirs*. There is only a small chance of it happening, but we should still be careful."

As Molvi Sirajul-Haq was speaking, Molvi Salimullah was handing an envelope to each soldier, with a bulge of money clearly visible inside. "By today's information, you each get a good 400,000 rupees. Per count it would have actually been 25,000 per person less, giving you only 375,000 each. But the way we are getting good news, it looks like you all will get even more of an increase in the future. Just pray that there will be delays instead of darkness in His world."

After saying this, he called everyone inside, where numerous dishes had been placed on the dinner mat.

Molvi Salimullah picked up a plate of sweets and said to everyone, "First have sweets on the success of this mission, and then dinner."

Molvi Sirajul-Haq laughed loudly. "Yes, brothers. It's a special occasion. Today we'll eat dessert before dinner!"

Everyone began to laugh. Idrees was already full after seeing the number of bills in his envelope. He slowly patted his pockets, smiled, and said: "Yes, Molvi sahib, let's fill up our stomachs as well, or our pockets will get jealous!"

Everyone enjoyed the joke and laughed more.

After dinner began, they talked about other topics. The room was full of the noise of clattering cutlery and jokes.

It was 4:00 am when they started leaving Molvi Sirajul-Haq's home. As Molvi Salimullah began to walk out the door, he said to Idrees,

"*Bhai*, in a few minutes, the *fajr* prayer is going to start. Why not go to the mosque, first?"

Idrees joined him, and on the way he mentioned Usman's illness to Molvi Salimullah, who said, "A strange man you are, Idrees. Your child is sick, and you haven't even told me or Molvi Sirajul-Haq *bhai*! He's a learned religious scholar. He could have told you the verses right now to treat him.

"But it's fine. Don't be worried. Let's pray the *fajr* and go to your home. I will try some verses. If he doesn't get better, I know some other religious healers who can be contacted and we'll see if it is helpful. Brother, there is a description of *jina* in Quran. But there are also verses too, which could break their evil spirits. *Allah Tabarak'Tallah* Himself has revealed in the Quran that we were the ones who created diseases and we are the ones who have also created the treatments. Let's go to the mosque first, and then to your home, okay? Don't worry, brother Idrees. *Allah Tabarak'Tallah* shall heal our son, Usman."

After a while, their car entered Shah Faisal Colony through Shahrah-e Faisal. They were just crossing through the railway line when they heard priests clearing their throats before sounding the Azan from neighbouring mosques. In no time, the air of Shah Faisal Colony was full of the echo of the Azan.

The entire area was asleep except for a couple of wandering dogs, which were growling and fighting over scraps of leftover meat around the carts across the street. A few drug addicts were also lying there, covered by small blankets torn and smeared with dirt.

There were no other cars other than the one Molvi Salimullah and Idrees were in.

When they crossed the same square of Shah Faisal Colony near the road of Musjid-e-Dinyat, Idrees suddenly had a flashback to when he burnt the *kafir* Christian alive. The one who bad-mouthed Muhammad, peace be upon him.

Idrees' gaze fell through the store and down to the footpath, stopping at the broken wall from where Usman had been watching the burning scene.

The car had barely reached the street of the mosque when two policemen walked out in front of them, raising a hand to stop.

Molvi Salimullah cursed under his breath and stopped the car.

One policeman looked into the window. He turned to his partner. "Oh, this is our Molvi Salimullah and Brother Idrees!"

Once Molvi Salimullah saw Constable Rahimdad, he stroked his beard and said, *"Walaikum-Assalam rahmatullahi."*

Hearing this, Rahimdad felt embarrassed and immediately replied, *"Assalamualaikum*-Rahmatullahi, Molvi sahib. How are you? It's been a long time. Everything okay?"

Molvi Salimullah looked Rahimdad in the eyes and said, "Yes, brother. We were out for good deeds of Allah and are now intending for the *fajr* prayer. You want to come? Idrees *bhai* is also with us."

"Oh, Idrees brother. How is everything?" Rahimdad turned to Idrees and shook hands with him.

"I'm good, Rahimdad *bhai.* How are you? How's everything at home?" Idrees said with a smile.

"My wife told me last night that your child was sick and she was actually in the same hospital because of her appendix pain. The doctor was suggesting surgery."

Rahimdad had started chatting with Idrees as if they were old pals.

"Allah grant her health…"

"Idrees *bhai* is also quite worried about his child' health," Salimullah interrupted. "And wanted to go back to his home and read some verses for healing."

"Oh, Molvi sahib, do tell us as well. My wife could finally feel better. She's been taking bottles of medicine 12 months a year."

Rahimdad had asked, so Molvi Salimullah replied:

"Sure, sure, *bhai*! Don't miss your prayers. The *namaz* has a lot of blessings."

"Yes, of course, Molvi sahib. I'll start praying more. For now, I only pray on Fridays. To be honest, sometimes we miss those as well…what can I do? Duty asks for day and night shifts both," Rahimdad said, looking at the ground.

"Oh, brother. The *namaz* is a duty of God, which is far bigger than your police duty. Understand?" Molvi Salimullah said loudly, stroking his beard again. "Let's go, Idrees. We'll miss our prayer."

Rahimdad gave a sigh of relief. "Okay, brother. Goodbye!"

"Goodbye." Saying this, Molvi Salimullah drove past the police officers.

After they left, constable Rahimdad turned to the other policeman and winked with a smile. "You recognize them? It's Molvi Salimullah, from Sipah-e Sahaba. They have high connections. Idrees is now also one of their men."

"Leave 'em. These are big people. We catch our small fish. Let's go over there, behind the carts."

Saying this, Rahimdad's partner cut him short, grabbing his belt and pulling him to the other side in a friendly way.

The sound of their laughter and the barking of the dogs over the leftover meat merged together and echoed in the darkness.

Chapter 28

Time: 7:30 pm
Date: November 27, 2016
Location: Mississauga, Canada

Sania held a cup of tea in her hand and sat next to Daleep in the living room. Both of them, quietly sipping tea, watched the weather forecast on the TV. After just a while, Daleep's other hand slowly moved to hold Sania's hand lovingly. They continued to sip tea quietly and watch the weather.

Both of them were currently being rained upon in their own weather. Their tears had been dried by now, but their hearts were still numb. It was a mixed feeling of happiness and sadness, but not a complete form of either. There was just a pulse instead of a heart, and just a soul instead of a body, which was living on that pulse.

Sania was still entrapped in the friction of Daleep's words spoken on the balcony.

Far away somewhere, behind the clouds, the raining of a strange emotion was still present, in which every drop was filled with the seas of love. She and Daleep were both drenched after standing in it for so long.

All the colours of the universe had been concealed in one waterfall and had joined with one another to resolve all the differences in colour.

All the weathers of the universe had been concealed in one waterfall and had joined with one another to resolve all the differences in weather.

All the sounds of the universe had been concealed in one waterfall and had joined with one another to resolve all the differences in sound…

…and had created one sound.

The song of love.

Sania and Daleep were watching TV, but were truly listening to the forecast inside of them.

They were quietly sitting inside themselves, getting a spiritual experience of love by taking out their soul from bodies rusted with colour, race and religion. Their fingers were slowly playing with each other, a touch not from their bodies but from their love.

They were both lost in each other, not knowing themselves, free of judgement from bodies, free from worldly contamination, quiet, alone and lost, like an element of love above the skies…indifferent to the traditional concept of God. Immersed in efforts to embrace the whole universe into one with the highest attributes, without any regret.

Suddenly, the chain of thought was broken. Daleep placed his cup of tea on the table and looked in Sania's eyes and smiled.

Sania asked Daleep quietly, "Have you been thinking what I have been thinking?"

"What were you thinking?"

"…that I don't want to betray love." Sania said, looking at Daleep.

"…and I have decided that I will leave Islam and adopt the Sikh religion."

"But why? I never asked you to change your religion. Nor did Abbaji. Beji doesn't know anything about this matter…then why are you talking about leaving your religion?" Daleep asked, surprised.

"Daleep, I've been thinking about this matter for two to three days, after your meeting with mom and dad. I can't live without you. I don't want anything except Daleep. Love, in its essence, is very selfish...as I am for you. Whatever you are: Hindu, Sikh, Christian or Muslim, when I fell in love with you, I didn't find you in the sayings of *Ramayan* or the verses of Quran. Your mother tongue was Punjabi, but you expressed your love in that language. Your religion was Sikh, and mine was Islam, but the destiny of both of them was only love. When race and religion pass through the body and reach the soul, they are left with nothing but love. Which is what I have with you. I don't know what I'm saying, but I'd never desire for you to become Muslim for my sake. Because if that happens, then I'll be betraying love."

After listening to all of this, Daleep opened his mouth, but Sania placed a finger on his lips. "No. Don't say anything, please. Just feel as though we haven't had a word together. After all, when two spirits talk to each other, the bodies don't get to speak."

These thoughts of Sania broke from spoken words, spread themselves into different colours, fell into musical notes and were lost in the air, travelling back two decades...

...reaching a certain underdeveloped area of Kabul, Afghanistan, and then turning themselves into a smile on the crying face of Sofia, who was holding Wahidi's hand tightly.

Chapter 29

Time: 12:00 Noon
Date: November 28, 2016
Location: Washington, USA

By the time Wahidi reached the end of *My Stroke of Insight*, the plane still had a few hours left until it reached New York. That's when the passenger sitting beside him asked, "So…are you a writer? A scholar?"

Wahidi smiled. "What made you think that?"

"For the entire flight, you've been busy reading books and writing down notes. I didn't want to disturb you, but since we're almost there, I thought I'd ask."

"Well, I don't know about scholar, but you can call me a writer. I've written a few books…mostly on political subjects. My name is Wahidi, and I am a professor at Kabul University in Afghanistan."

"Oh, it's an honour to sit with someone of such a profound background. My name is Anand. I've been studying social sciences at Columbia University." The passenger gestured to the book. "Jill Bolte Taylor's work. I've read it and was very impressed. Most likely because I'm from India, and Indians are very spiritual. How do you like it, with a background of political science?"

Wahidi scratched his head. "Well, the writer used research about the differences between the left and the right brain to explain the peculiar experience of a stroke she had. For her, the left part of her brain, the 'mechanical' part, was damaged because of the stroke. The right part had dominated by expressing its innate spiritual feelings. Reading this with a social-scientific background…to describe that we'd have to go into human history.

"Centuries ago, back when we all lived in caves, human insecurities created the concepts of God and tribal property: meaning religion and nationalism, so we could fight back against enemies from sky and land. In an economic era, the modern world understood science and developed secular societies to resolve the negative consequences from religion, developing political methods and strengthening their national benefits. Meanwhile, underdeveloped nations never understood the difference between the left and right brain, and instead of coming out of the primitive state, are still stuck in the jungle of the right side, conveniently entangled and utilized for selfish reasons by their corrupt political and religious leaders."

An announcement came over the plane's public address. "Ladies and gentlemen, we will be reaching JFK Airport in half an hour. Please make sure your seat belt is securely fastened…"

Wahidi took a deep breath. "Finally, we're here."

Anand offered his phone number before they parted ways. He was interested in hearing Wahidi's lecture at the University of Washington and was intent on meeting him again.

Once Wahidi reached Washington, he spent a day getting over jet lag. The next day when he woke up, he called his old friends first. He had a lot of friends in America. Sherazi, a friend from university times, was living in New Jersey. Sherazi was the one who reached Bamiyan after Masood's attack and found him brutally injured. He had quickly spread a false rumour—that Wahidi had also been killed alongside his parents and girlfriend—and then took Wahidi to Zahedan, Iran, to the home of a family friend.

Sherazi's children had already grown up, and he was a grandfather now. He was quite excited when he heard his friend was coming to the States. He was continuously in contact with Wahidi, having had read his books and articles, and also commenting on his blog sometimes. Wahidi had promised that after the lecture he would be staying with him for a few days so they could sit together and talk about the past.

Wahidi was surprised to find that he was the only one invited from Afghanistan. There were scholars and political analysts from India, Pakistan, Bangladesh and Nepal and from Central Asia to discuss this important topic from the Eastern part of the world.

The next few days flew past very quickly, as he was busy in his room completing his article or having discussions with different professors. He never realized that his name had become so respected over the last twenty years of his writing career. His secular thoughts had given him academic value—perhaps that was the reason that the University of California had picked his name without any reference or relation—directly requesting the chancellor of Kabul University to permit the lecture.

The day of the seminar, the room was full of hundreds of attendees. A live TV recording of the event had been arranged, and many newspaper reporters were present. Most of the attendees were university students, who, through their appearance, showed connections to numerous races and religions.

When Wahidi finished his lecture, the room reverberated with sounds of clapping for a minute before open dialogue began.

A Saudi student stood up, wearing a *thobe* and a *ghutra*. "Sir, after joining the global village, won't Afghanistan lose its cultural identity?"

"Culture was created by human beings. If a new culture develops from the cross of the West and the East, it becomes a mosaic of culture for all of humanity. Wouldn't a mosaic culture be a better identity? If a peculiar culture's recognition develops distances through negativity, then wouldn't you give priority to nearness over farness?"

Wahidi's reply made the Saudi student think, but he quickly recovered and fired back more questions.

"…but identity is in human psychology. And without it, how would a human introduce himself? Don't you think that religion has replaced culture in terms of introduction? Isn't globalization just a Western conspiracy to spread their culture across the world?"

"No," Wahidi said with similar confidence. "First of all, globalization hasn't developed any restrictions on the members of any society for their customs, values or religions. Look around yourself. You see students from Nepal, Sudan, Saudi Arabia, Iran, Canada, Europe. You can easily recognize them by their colour, customs and appearance. Religion is a spiritual issue of human beings, so we need to keep it in our hearts as an identity of our souls, rather than our bodies. If we get rid of the artificial concept of nationalism through globalization, wouldn't it be good?

"I'm not telling you that you were Pakistani yesterday and should become American today, but I'm saying that you should get freedom from the judgement of colour, race and religion. Just become a citizen of the global religion: humanism. Just become a speaker of the global language. Just live under one umbrella, with all of your identity…all of your values, language and religion, with all of your tolerance that comes from recognizing other human beings like you. I believe that behaviour of non-tolerance makes us no different from animals."

A young woman raised her hand from the back of the crowd.

"Sir, don't you think that religion and nationalism are innate human characteristics? How do we get rid of them if they are that natural?"

Wahidi looked at the girl. Her face was familiar to him.

"When animals are born in a place, they naturally fall in love with that place, whether it be a cave, a mountain, a jungle or a pond. Even if animals are confined in a cage for a long time, they begin to love that cage. If you forcefully take that place away from them, they show sadness. That's the same feeling that we human beings had with our caves during the Stone Age. Animals also have spirituality in their feelings, like the sadness you find in the eyes of a mother deer when you snatch her child. You'll find that this is the same love in dogs that has been developed for human beings, which is pure; it hasn't been polluted with the socio-political side of religion. For us, it has been polluted. We need to learn the difference of this innate character from that of animals. The lack of this consciousness develops violence in us."

After listening to the reply, a Sikh student sitting next to the girl raised his hand. "But, sir, how can you say whether these actions were developed through the evolutionary process? Maybe they were nurtured, not natural."

Wahidi gave him a smile, "The right side of the brain creates art, music, spirituality, loyalty, and love. But when this love and loyalty steps through the mechanical stairs of colour, race and religion—the left side of the brain—it turns into either a good or a bad shape, according to the environment it grows in. If it is an economically weak society, and people aren't educated from a modern world with scientific change, then their weak values develop violence. This violence develops a negative, vicious circle, in which the entire generation is trapped and ultimately develops a collective suicide. The ethical values of good and bad are connected with their consciousness of time and space, so it isn't absolute, but totally relative."

When Wahidi paused to take a breath, the girl sitting next to the Sikh student raised her hand again:

"How is self-consciousness possible in this era?"

"We have to break the artificial wall with our conscious efforts responsible for creating our defences. We have to recognize the political and economic agenda, creating connections between spirituality and religion or patriotism and nationalism, because intentionally or unintentionally, this agenda is the reason of the contamination of hatred within love."

After he finished, the girl started clapping and then, one by one, the entire hall reverberated with the sound of clapping once again.

After the seminar, Wahidi was standing on the side with a cup of tea in hand, talking with other speakers. He heard a voice behind him.

"Sir?"

Wahidi turned around and saw that the girl who asked the question and the boy wearing a turban were standing there. Wahidi shook his hand. "I was impressed with your intelligent questions!"

The girl replied, "Professor Wahidi, we are very pleased to meet you. My name is Sania, and this is my boyfriend, Daleep. We came here from Toronto to see you."

Wahidi hugged both of them. After the seminar, Wahidi, Sania, and Daleep spent the afternoon together. The three of them had dinner and talked for a long time. Sania thought that he should come to Canada so that he could spend some time with them, but Wahidi only had a visa for England and America, and he could only get a Canadian one from Kabul.

Sania and Daleep showed concern about the attacks on him:

"There's a lot of danger to your life in Afghanistan…you really shouldn't go to back. The American government will easily offer you political asylum."

Wahidi smiled and replied, "I have looked into that, but I'd rather to go back to Afghanistan. I'm like the protector of our new generation there. My students are my coming tomorrow. They are the rays of my light…spreading it like the sun. If I don't sacrifice today, I fear that tomorrow the Sofia inside me will ask, 'Today in Afghanistan, does a Masood stop his sister from creating art? Today in Afghanistan, does a Masood stop his sister from getting an education? Today in Afghanistan, is a Masood still killing his own sister with his own hands? Can a Sunni Sofia fall in love with a Shia Agha-Khani?' Maybe tomorrow, standing on the podium, I might be able to answer all of your questions, but not a single question from the Sofia inside of me."

After saying this, Wahidi wiped his eyes and said, "That's why, my friends, I'll have to go back. I'll return here, because in this new global world, where we have people collected from different races and religions, we should know the answers to their conflicts. The difference between them and Afghanistan is that they are living in a two different geographical worlds, and I have a dream of a global world for that geographical world."

Wahidi waved to the waiter and asked for the bill.

Leaving Wahidi in the lobby, Sania and Daleep told him that they were staying at a friend's home for now and had a flight the next day.

As Daleep and Sania's car took an exit for the highway, Sania's cell phone rang. On the other end was her mother.

"Sania, your dad wants me to ask you about what Daleep has decided…?"

"Yes, mom. Daleep said that he's ready to become a Muslim for me…" Then she completed her sentence casually, "…but mom, I also have the same opinion. I can change to Sikh and leave Islam. But today we have decided that to be one, we don't need any change."

"What do you mean," Her mother asked. "Are you going to leave him and come home?"

"No. Mom, we're going to live together and marry each other. He'll be a Sikh and I'll be a Muslim."

On the other side, her mother buried her face in her hands. "…and tomorrow, your kids? What about them?"

"They'll decide about their religion and nationality after growing up in the light of their education and consciousness," Sania replied in the same peaceful tone.

"Okay, Mom. Daleep and I had come to Washington to attend a seminar. Tomorrow we'll be back in Toronto, and then we'll talk about it. Say my salaam to Dad." When she finished, Sania turned off her phone.

After a few minutes, both of their hands moved and held each other.

Chapter 30

Time: 12:00 Noon
Date: November 29, 2016
Location: Shah Faisal Colony, Karachi, Pakistan

Molvi Salimullah had been trying to treat Usman for the past few days by reciting Quranic verses, but unfortunately the boy had become no better. Most of the time he was sleeping because of the tranquilizers prescribed to him by the doctors but then he would wake himself up with a hysteric scream. Sometimes he was fine, while other times his anxiety became worse. It was hard to say if the medicines were doing him any good.

One day, Molvi Salimullah, tired, took Idrees aside and said, "Brother Idrees, I have a feeling that this spirit has a very strong influence over Usman. Why don't you see another spiritual healer? I know someone who is experienced in this work. I'll give you his address. Use my name when you meet him, and he probably won't charge you much. Still, Brother, be sure to leave a thousand rupees in his hands — you know everyone needs money, and Brother, when the wallet brings in money, the heart sends out prayers."

With the last statement, a smile spread itself on Molvi Salimullah's face. Bakhtawar had insisted on him staying for breakfast, and in a few minutes they were sitting and eating omelettes and *parathas*.

While Molvi Salimullah and Idrees were eating breakfast, Bakhtawar was speaking from the side of the kitchen so that she could adhere to Islamic culture all the while making sure Molvi Salimullah wouldn't feel as though he were a guest.

"These omelettes are tasty," Molvi Salimullah said, looking towards the kitchen.

"Thank you, Molvi sahib." Bakhtawar said. "The day you first came to our home. Ever since that day, Allah has been blessing us again and again. Idrees has devoted himself to the mosque…"

Molvi Salimullah interrupted: "The way Brother Idrees has been working, Molvi Sirajul-Haq sahib has decided to award him the responsibility of a couple madrassas in Punjab. We decided last night that he should go and visit Punjab for a few days. Actually, he should be leaving tomorrow. It has become quite urgent now… you don't have any objections, do you?"

"Oh, of course not, Molvi sahib. For Idrees to be chosen to do these noble deeds…it's but another gift from Allah." Bakhtawar replied, impressed.

"Then it's settled, Brother Idrees. You've already decided, so get ready. I think you should buy the ticket today for a better seat…and yes, remember to fly first class."

Bakhtawar remembered something and said, "But, Molvi sahib, Usman is sick! How will I take care of him without Idrees?"

Idrees interrupted, "Molvi sahib, why don't we take Usman and Bakhtawar to the spiritual healer right now, so we can get some prayers? Afterwards, I'll leave both of them at my aunt's, and then we can arrange tickets to Punjab."

"Yes, that's good." Molvi Salimullah wiped his mouth with a handkerchief and took a final sip of his cup of tea. "All right, Idrees *bhai*, I'll take my leave."

After Molvi Salimullah left, Idrees locked the door and pulled out a fat stack of cash. When he put it in Bakhtawar's hands, her eyes widened. "Let's go inside," Idrees said to Bakhtawar.

Once they were inside the room, Idrees looked at Bakhtawar and said: "Look, this is the money Molvi Sirajul-Haq sent through Molvi Salimullah. He says I should leave as soon as possible to organize the madrassas in Punjab."

Idrees was satisfied with Molvi Salimullah's cleverness. He had made a brilliant excuse for him to leave Karachi, relieving Idrees of having to make up a new story. Idrees had already estimated that the attack last week had killed a good number of *kafir*s. With a calculation of 25,000 rupees per body, Idrees would get over 100,000 before leaving Punjab.

When Idrees reached the roundabout, he put Usman onto the ground and said to Bakhtawar,

"You stay here. Let me arrange a taxi so we can head to the spiritual healer."

He turned, and he saw Kallo and Rab Nawaz, sitting with their knees folded on a wall, watching the girls walking down the road.

When Idrees saw them, he yelled, waving his hands: "Oy! Rab Nawaz *bhai. Assalamualaikum-warahmatullahi-wabarakatuh.*"

When Rab Nawaz saw him, he jumped off of the wall and headed towards Idrees. Behind him, Kallo followed.

"Everything good, Rab Nawaz *bhai*?"

"Yeah, everything's fine. I was thinking about visiting you a couple times, but you've become some sort of hero. It's so difficult to find you…you're never home or in the bazaar," Rab Nawaz complained.

"Nah, brother. It's just that Molvi Salimullah has given us a lot of responsibilities…the entire day just goes by. On top of that, I have to oversee the mosques too. That's why I'm so busy all the time. Okay, listen." Idrees said, lowering his tone. "There haven't been any *kafir* issues around here, right? Look, we need to keep an eye on these *kafir*…*Shias* and *Ahmadis*. They're the real enemies of our Islam. I now realize how badly they've messed up our religion."

Kallo, hearing this, came near Idrees and said, "*Bhai*, I've said this to Rab Nawaz before—there's a new store nearby. The owner is an Ahmadi *kafir*."

Kallo pointed at a small shoe shop at the corner of the roundabout.

"Really!" Idrees said, shocked. "How'd this guy get into our neighborhood? Doesn't he know that this area belongs to Molvi Salimullah, from Musjid-e-Dinyat?"

Kallo shrugged and said, "Okay, Brother Idrees. What're we going to do?"

Idrees looked into their eyes and said, "Come on, let's introduce ourselves now, so that he can get out of here." Idrees, Rab Nawaz and Kallo left the corner and headed to the new shoe shop by the roundabout.

This shop happened to be near the same place where months ago Idrees had burned and killed a Christian blamed for blasphemy. When Bakhtawar saw Idrees leaving, she softly called out to him, "Usman is getting quite restless!"

"Oh," Idrees waved. "I'll be back in just a couple of minutes." They walked into the new shop and found a young boy busy bringing shoes from the showcase to a customer. The shop was brand new, and on one wall the shoes had been freshly polished and arranged.

The shop was decorated with statues at each corner. There was the model of a shoe made of plaster of Paris.

A line of chairs ran down the middle, where a few customers were sitting and waiting for their turn. A middle-aged man sat at the register, sporting a French-cut beard and quietly reading a newspaper.

He was most likely the owner of the shop, as a framed picture of *Mirza Ghulam Ahmad* hung behind him on the wall. The photo was black and white, and could be recognized at a glance. From a distance it looked like a photo cut from the newspaper.

Idrees looked around the store and walked up to the owner.

"So, what's going on here?" Idrees demanded, scratching his beard.

"Uh…how can I help you?" The man in the French-cut beard replied.

"We'll be the ones helping you. Whose photo is this?" Idrees pointed to the portrait.

"A photo of *Masih Maud.*" He said, frowning. Perhaps he had judged the intentions of Idrees and his friends.

"So…am I going to throw this out, or are you going to do it?" Idrees stared into the man's eyes.

"*Bhai*, the only reason we put this picture up was for blessings from Allah. Nothing else," The man said in an apologetic tone.

"You *Qadiani*?" Idrees spoke loudly this time.

"Yes…I'm Ahmadi, and I believe in God."

Idrees shouted, "Okay…say this loudly: Muhammad, peace be upon him, is the last Prophet of Allah."

The man said, "Uh…why are you doing all of this? I believe in Allah, and have faith in Muhammad, peace be upon him. Now, could you kindly please leave?"

The young boy who had been busy taking a customer's size walked over. "What's happening here, Daddy?" He looked at Rab Nawaz and Idrees.

"If you'd really like a blessing, then put up a photo of Allah and Muhammad's name! If not, then put up a photo of the *kabba* and the Nabvi Mosque!

"What is this nonsense?" Idrees grabbed the man's collar and tossed him aside. He stepped up onto a stool and ripped out the picture.

The son of the owner got angry, screaming "What is this behaviour?"

As soon as the words left his mouth, Rab Nawaz slapped him, causing him to bleed from his cheek.

When Idrees saw this, he joined the action. Flipping over a chair, he kicked the man in the stomach. In the meantime, Kallo smashed the glass of the showcases and threw the shoes out of the store. Shocked by this sudden attack, the owner and his son stumbled outside, shouting for help. Kallo, Idrees and Rab Nawaz chased after them.

"Kill these *Qadiani kafir*s!" Idrees yelled.

"They don't call our Beloved Prophet the last Prophet! How dare they have the nerve to run their business here, in a Muslim community?" Kallo punched the man in the back, sending him barrelling forward into the dirt.

When his son ran over and tried to help his father, Idrees kicked him too, screaming, "Get out of here, you pigs!" He pushed the son over once more.

Hearing the noise, people gathered around the scene, running out of their stores and homes. People sitting in the square rushed towards the roadside where Idrees, Rab Nawaz and Kallo were beating both shopkeepers horribly.

After the explosion of violence a month ago, most of the people there assumed that there had been another case of blasphemy.

Some people had started to chant. "Nar-e Takbeer, *Allahu akbar!*" Others had already started to loot the store.

When Bakhtawar saw Idrees, she started running towards him, worried. In all of the commotion, Usman had slipped his fingers from Bakhtawar's hands and had frantically run back, looking for somewhere to hide. Terrified, Bakhtawar had forgotten about Usman and had run to where Idrees, Rab Nawaz, and Kallo were assaulting the men, who were covered in mud, dirt and blood.

Bakhtawar screamed, grabbing Idrees from behind and pulling him back. "Idrees, leave them! Stop it!"

But Idrees was overcome by anger. His face was flushed with rage. He was barely going to leave them alive.

Finally, he stopped beating them. Taking a step back, he spit on them, yelling curses.

"You dogs! Before you die a horrible death from my hands, get yourselves out of here! Your *kafiri* business isn't going to run here! Close all of this shit down and leave our place in forty-eight hours."

He looked up at Kallo and Rab Nawaz, who were still hitting their victims. "Leave them, Rab Nawaz. Let the dogs go. Kallo, let's go. Don't know where they come from…"

Idrees ran a hand through his hair and pushed his way out of the crowd. Behind him, Rab Nawaz and Kallo walked out as well. Both of the victims were lying on the footpath, shrieking in pain. Instead of taking them to the hospital, people were standing around making videos with their phones.

Leaving the rush, Idrees thought of Usman. He shouted to Bakhtawar. "Oy, where'd our Usman go? I left him with you."

Bakhtawar turned and looked around anxiously. Idrees started running here and there, trying to find his son amongst the crowd. Usman wasn't there. There was chaos everywhere. The crowd was busy watching the drama.

Idrees turned to Bakhtawar in anger. "Who told you to get in the middle of a men's scrap? I told you to watch over Usman! Instead, you…"

That's when Idrees heard Rab Nawaz yelling to him. "Idrees *bhai*, Usman's over here!"

Idrees and Bakhtawar ran over to where Rab Nawaz was standing behind the broken wall…from where Usman, frightened, was watching the violence through a crack.

When Idrees and Bakhtawar reached the wall and spread their arms open, Usman cringed back, terrified, and started to cry.

Idrees and Bakhtawar stared around. Many more children sat behind the broken wall, tears in their eyes and fear on their faces.

Vocabulary

Ababeel Birds — According to a Quranic story, the Ababeel birds saved the Kaaba from an attack from Abraha, king of Yemen.

Agarbatti — An incense stick traditionally used in Islamic ceremonies.

Ahle Sunnat Wal Jama'at — A Sunni sect of Islam.

Ahmadis — Practicers of a sect of Islam that believes Mirza Ghulam Ahmad was the promised Messiah

Alhamdulillah — Expression in Islamic conversations. Literally means "Praise be to Allah."

Allah miyah — usually used when referring to God with love

Allah Tabarak'Tallah — An honorific way to mention Allah.

Allah-Hu Akbar — An Islamic phrase, meaning "Allah is the greatest."

Assalamualaikum — Muslim greeting. Commonly treated like "hello," it literally means "God bless you."

Barelvi — Practicers of a Sunni sect of Islam that believes in the Barelvi school of thought.

Bhagwan — Hindi word for God.

bhai — common slang for "bro" in Pakistan

Biryani — A South Asian rice dish, with meat, vegetables, dry fruit, etc.

Bolani — An Afghani dish consisting of bread stuffed with potatoes.

Burqa — An outer garment worn by women in some Islamic countries.

Charpai — A traditional woven bed mostly used in warm areas. Also originated from India & Pakistan.

Daal — An Indian-Pakistani dish consisting of split lentils.

Daesh — Arabic name for the Islamic State of Iraq and Syria (ISIS).

Dallip Kumar — An iconic Bollywood superstar.

Deobandi — Practicers of a Sunni sect of Islam that believes in the Deobandi school of thought.

Deobandi maslak — The Sunni sect of Islam that believes in the Deobandi school of thought.

Dupatta — Scarf worn over the shoulder by Muslim women.

Fajr — Morning Islamic prayer before the sun rises.

Gajar-Ka-Halwa — A dessert made up of carrots

Ghazi — An Islamic warrior who goes out to battle and comes back alive.

Ghutra — A middle-eastern headdress also worn by men.

Gulbuddin Hekmatyar — an Afghan politician, founder of the Hezb-e Islami political party

Hadith — The documented reports of particular sayings and actions from Prophet Muhammad

Heretic — A book by a Somalian-born Dutch-American writer, Ayaan Hirsi Ali. It compared Muhammad's life in Mecca, where he was born and spread his message, and his life in Medina, where he migrated and fought back against his enemies.

Hezb-e Islami — An Islamic political party in Afghanistan, influenced by the Muslim Brotherhood of Egypt

Hijab — The head covering worn in public by some Muslim women.

Inshallah — Used by Muslims to start a task, literally means "If Allah wills it."

Isha Prayer — A prayer practiced by Muslims after the sun sets.

Jamat ud Dawa — An extremist Islamic organization in Pakistan led by Hafiz Muhammad Saeed.

Jazāk-Allāh — Literally means "May Allah reward you with greatness."

Jihad — A struggle or fight against the enemies of Islam.

Jihadis — People who participate in jihad.

Kaaba — The most sacred site in Islam.

Kafir — Another term for "infidel."

Kafir-ki-olad — Common street slang. Literally calling someone "son of an Infidel."

Kafir saaley — Common street slang, directly insulting someone by calling him an Infidel.

Kalma-e-tayyaba — The first of the six declarations of faith in Islam

Kalma-e-shahadat — The second of the six declarations of faith in Islam

Kandil Lamp — A small lantern used for light in places where electricity isn't available.

Karbala — A historic place in Iraq where Muhammad's grandson, Husayn Ibn Ali, was killed.

Korma — A dish containing meat, vegetables, yogurt and other spices. Popular in the Indian subcontinent.

Kufr — infidelity

Kurta Shalwar — Sort of baggy pyjamas, common wear in Pakistan.

Lashkar-e-tayyaba — One of the largest Islamic militant organizations in South Asia, operating mainly from Pakistan.

Lassi — A popular traditional yogurt-based milk drink in the Indian Subcontinent.

Madrassa — A school where mostly Islamic subjects are taught, such as interpreting the Quran, Islamic law, and the Arabic language.

Mahram — A woman's mahram is a person whom she is never permitted to marry because of a close blood relationship. Literally means "Prohibited."

Mard-e-Momin Mard-e-Haq — A title for General Muhammad Zia-ul-Haq, former president of Pakistan. Literally means "an ideal Muslim man."

Masha'Allah — Used for expressing appreciation in the Arabic language. Literally means "God has willed."

Masih Maud — A title for Mirza Ghulam Ahmad, literally means "successor of the Messiah."

Mazar — Tomb for Muslim personalities.

Milad Sharif — Celebration of the birthday of Prophet Muhammad

Mirza Ghulam Ahmad — The successor of the Messiah, the prophet in the Ahmadi sect of Islam.

Miyan — Used to address someone with respect.

Molvi — One with an extensive knowledge of Islam.

Mullah — A person qualified from an Islamic school.

Na-mahram — A woman's mahram is a person whom she is permitted to marry. Literally means "Allowed."

Naan — A flatbread popular around India and Pakistan.

Nauzubillah — An Arabic word Muslims say before saying something negative. Literally means "I seek refuge in Allah."

Nikha — An Islamic legal contract between a husband and wife.

Paan — an after-dinner treat consisting of a betel leaf filled with chopped Areca nuts. It is chewed for its stimulant and psychoactive effects.

Paratha — A flatbread popular around India and Pakistan, made with oil.

Qadiani — Another name for Ahmadis.

Qawwalis — a form of Sufi devotional music, popular in South Asia.

Rab-ul-Izzat — An hhonorific way to mention Allah.

Ramayan — An ancient Indian poem narrating the endeavor of the prince Rama to rescue his wife Sita. Combined with the Mahabharata, it forms the Hindu Itihasa.

Roti — A flatbread originating from the Indian subcontinent.

Rukū — Bowing down as part of the Islamic prayer.

Sahaba-Ikram — A companion of the Islamic prophet Muhammad.

Saira Bano — An iconic Bollywood superstar, wife of Dallip Kumar.

Solsol and Shahmama — Two prominent statues of Buddha in Afghanistan.

Sawab — An Islamic reward for a noble job.

Seekh Kebabs — A dish from Indian cuisine, consisting of a mixture of minced meat.

Seerat-e Mustaqeem — The correct path to a righteous task from Allah.

Shab-e barat — A Muslim event that is regarded as the night Allah decides whether a person is to live or die in the coming year as well as the night Allah forgives sinners.

Sharia Law — Islamic legal laws.

Shias — After Sunni, the biggest sect of Islam.

Subḥān-Allāh — In Islam, traditionally used when appreciating Allah's creation. Literally means, "Praise be to Allāh."

Sunnat — The teachings, deeds and sayings, permissions or disapprovals of the Islamic prophet Muhammad.

Sūrat Al-Tawbah — The ninth chapter of the Quran.

Tahsellat-e Ali Islam — The name of a well-known building on the Kabul highway.

Tasbi — A small string of beads used when repeatedly reciting short phrases or prayers, either silently within the mind or aloud.

Thobe — A Saudi-Arabian garment worn by men.

Turban — A headdress worn by Sikh-Indians.

Ummah — The concept of a Muslim brotherhood in India or Pakistan.

Waalaikumsalam — Muslim response to Assalamualaikum. Literally means "God bless you as well."

Wahabi — The Sunni sect of Islam.

About the Author:

Baland Iqbal practices Internal Medicine in Ontario, and is currently the Chief Hospitalist at Norfolk General Hospital. Other than writing Urdu fiction, he enjoys philosophical, political, social and psychological topics for discussion in South Asian TV channels in Canada. He is the author of many books of Urdu fiction, including Angel's Tears, My 51 Short Stories and All of my Love Letters.

Reviews of the Urdu Language Version of Broken Wall:

Is loving a sin and killing in the name of a merciful God a virtue? Baland Iqbal asks this chilling question in the novel Broken Wall.

Baland Iqbal has a multifaceted personality. He is a writer and a doctor, a journalist and a humanist. He has already published two collections of short stories. Broken Wall is his first philosophical novel. In that novel when religious fundamentalism reaches its extreme a broken wall becomes a metaphor of decaying and fragile values. Members of the younger generation try to hide behind that wall.

Characters of the novel highlight that in the 21st century humanity is at the crossroads. Human beings have a choice individually and collectively. They can commit collective suicide by nuclear weapons or they can grow to the next stage of human evolution, learn to resolve conflicts and live in peace and harmony.

Baland Iqbal's novel is a mirror that reflects the dark as well as the bright side of humanity. Baland Iqbal has done some literary experiments in the novel. Because of his honesty, rather brutal honesty, Baland Iqbal might face some controversy and criticism by the conservative, religious and traditional segments of the community but that is the role literature plays. It challenges the regressive and unjust traditions of the society.

I congratulate Baland Iqbal for writing such a bold and timely novel and sharing his insights, foresights and hindsights.

Dr. Khalid Sohail
Psychiatrist

Baland Iqbal's ideological novel Broken Wall, in the Urdu language, captivated my emotions. The reading of the novel in its original genre made my eyes teary. The novel takes a reader on an intellectual journey from the medieval and archaic societies of Afghanistan and Pakistan to the modern, western societies of Canada and the USA, and forces one to think that a different cultural mix is a difficult proposition, which demands serious thinking. Where to go from here is another query to probe into.

The novel opens up some very sacred and hidden aspects of the human mind still living in medieval thinking, despite being Canadian. This novel is the first of its kind in Urdu literature. The flickering flame of intellectualism in Urdu literature, particularly in Pakistan, will definitely be fueled by Baland. I have no hesitation in saying that in the dying days of the world full of past-obscurantism over this ideological novel will go a long way.

Advocate Jawaid A. Siddiqui
Political Analyst